The Church That Glowed

BY

WYNELLE B. GARDNER

Drawings by Holly Zapp

LOGOS INTERNATIONAL
PLAINFIELD, NEW JERSEY

Citations from the Bible in this book are drawn from the following versions:

THE REVISED STANDARD VERSION OF THE BIBLE, © 1946, 1952, 1971, 1973 by the Division of Christian Education of the National Council of Churches of Christ in the United States of America. Used by permission. (Commonly abbreviated: RSV)

GOOD NEWS FOR MODERN MAN, THE NEW TESTAMENT IN TODAY'S ENGLISH VERSION, © 1966 by the American Bible Society. (Commonly abbreviated: TEV)

THE LIVING BIBLE PARAPHRASED, © 1971 by Tyndale House Publishers. (Commonly abbreviated: TLB)

THE KING JAMES VERSION (Commonly abbreviated: KJV)

THE CHURCH THAT GLOWED

© copyright 1976 by Logos International. All rights reserved
International Standard Book Number: 0–88270–128–2 (cloth)
                                      0–88270–129–0 (paper)
Library of Congress Catalog Card Number: 75-10243
Logos International, Plainfield, New Jersey 07061
Printed in the United States of America

Contents

THE CHURCH THAT GLOWED

CHAPTER ONE

The Prophecy of Jeremiah

SHAFTS OF light from the late afternoon sun slanted through the stained-glass windows of Bellview Presbyterian Church. On a Wednesday afternoon in January, 1975, the scarlet-carpeted sanctuary was quiet but not entirely deserted. Seated on the front pew on the west side of the church, five small mice and a mother mouse sat within a gem-like halo of suspended light. Directly in front of them, perched with great dignity on the pulpit, sat husband and father, Jeremiah Malachi Mouse. Lifelong residents of BPC, Jeremiah had called his family together to announce an event of utmost importance.

From left to right they sat, according to their ages: Mother Priscilla, next on her right was Timothy, the mouse equivalent of an eighteen-year-old boy. Next was Peter, seventeen; Phoebe, sixteen; John Mark, fourteen and Baby Mary, almost two. It was a lovely family, all bathed and polished until they shone like jewels. Or was it the heavenly radiance shining through the window? Jeremiah cleared his throat.

"Dearly beloved family, we are gathered together to receive a piece of news that may make a lot of difference in our lives, and certainly in the life of this church." He paused for effect just as he'd seen the Reverend Mr. Hanagan do for twelve years. Jeremiah's speech was a mixture of the Reverend Mr. H.'s sermons and that of the brash young assistant custodian, Tom Packney. It was a medley of two worlds: one holy and seventyish; the other worldly and teenish (seventeenish, to be exact). All of Jeremiah's education and that of his five children had been gained at BPC — *cum laude*, he would have said. After all, what else was there to do on long winter nights but gnaw one's way through six shelves of theological tomes? Mother Priscilla had been educated in a cathedral in Newark.

He went on. "I must admit I've seen this coming for some time. Scuttlebutt hath it that the Reverend Mr. Hanagan has retired. We all know he's been away for several weeks, but now *they* say," and he pointed downstairs in the general direction of the church offices, "that tomorrow a new minister arrives!"

As gently bred as the five little mice were, this piece of news set them all a-twitter. Tails thumped excitedly on the polished maple pew. High-pitched voices rose in nervous excitement. Phoebe developed a twitch in her left ear and John Mark took a forbidden nibble of a blue hymnal. Only Mrs. M. maintained a measure of composure, though her little pink tongue darted in and out.

Jeremiah had to rap for order. "Cool it, kids." Then he proceeded. "Verily I say unto you, he cometh tomorrow. His name is The Reverend Doctor Andrew Pinkham Mahoney. He's thirty-two, unmarried and arrives fresh from teaching the, ah, Philosophy of Inter-Personal Relationships at Wedgewood Divinity School." Jeremiah glanced at the notes he held in his hand. Even a graduate of BPC couldn't be expected to remember all those big words.

"The question is, will we be allowed to remain here in this our hallowed home, or will somebody blow our cover?"

Timothy, the eldest, held up his right front paw for recognition. Jeremiah said, "The chair recognizes the delegate from the Choir Loft."

"Papa," squeaked Timothy. "I think we have nothing to fear. You know how well we've concealed ourselves for years using our aliases. With each of us representing a different part of the church, I doubt if even the Reverend Doctor Mahoney will discover us."

"Yeah," chimed in John Mark. "He'll never find us!"

"I don't recall recognizing the cabinet member from the kitchen," Jeremiah harumphed.

"Oh, 'scuse me, Pop. I forgot to hold up my paw." After remedying that oversight, John Mark promptly was recognized and spoke out in his best Packney dialect.

"It's been real neat fooling all those ladies and people who come into the kitchen. Everytime they hear me squeak, I just turn up the light under their teakettle or give that rusty old can opener a twist, and they think it's their appliances!"

"I suppose my cover is really the best," said Timothy. "And virtually foolproof. I can sing at the top of my voice, and they think it's a malfunction of the organ. Oh, the times they've called the organ repair man. He's about to write them off as a bunch of nuts!"

Decently and in order, each mouse held up a paw and was recognized according to the department he or she represented. Peter, from the Library; Phoebe, from the secretary's Filing Cabinet and Baby Mary from the children's Nursery. Priscilla and Jeremiah alternated between the Pastor's Study and the Founder's Room. The latter they considered to be very appropriate, as they had arrived with the foundation material in 1958, and considered themselves founders in every sense of the word.

Each delegate gave his or her views on whether or not it was likely that the new minister would discover and oust the mouse family. Cabinet member Phoebe was the only one to cast a negative vote. This probably came from years of licking envelopes in the secretary's Filing Cabinet and from scurrying out from under the carbon paper. She always had purple streaks on her smooth brown fur and was probably the first mouse in town to have lavender frosting at the beauty salon.

"I'm sure he'll smoke us out if he's one of those theological biggies from the seminary." Phoebe sometimes liked to shock her conservative parents with rather loose language. She knew words even Tom Packney didn't use. She continued. "I think we'd better split. I hear there's an opening in that new beauty salon across the street. That's what I dig. Whatta ya say, gang?" Besides being sometimes crude, Phoebe was also rather vain.

Jeremiah felt he'd stumbled onto the answer. "Phoebe,

have you been frequenting the Youth Lounge and watching television?" By the blush on her smooth pink face, she admitted her guilt. However, they could pull out her toenails and cut off her cheese for a week, and she'd never tell how the mice from the Pharmacy came over every Wednesday night to help her turn on the TV and watch the violent movies. Never, never, never! A girl was entitled to some secrets, even in church.

Peter, the bookish mouse from the Library, adjusted his tiny, gold-rimmed glasses and spoke softly.

"Speak up, Peter. We can't hear you," his father said.

"I daresay we'll be safe enough, Pater, if we continue with our same *modus operandi*. If they should attempt harassment we could always put into effect the *lex talionis*."

"Oh, dear," sighed Priscilla. "Why don't you speak English?" She remembered how she thought Peter would never learn to talk and now that he had, she couldn't understand half of what he said.

"I meant, of course, the law of retaliation, Mater. We could retaliate, don't you know?"

Up to this time Baby Mary had participated little, mainly because she was having her four o'clock bottle. She gurgled once or twice, and the family understood what she meant. An untimely burp just now drew a very stern glance from Jeremiah. He asked for a motion to dismiss the meeting just as the elderly custodian, Mr. Walters, came in with his vacuum cleaner. From force of habit they all started to jump down from the pew, then they remembered that Mr. Walters didn't see well, didn't hear well and didn't smell well, so they felt quite safe enough and finished their meeting according to Robert's Rules of Order. Jeremiah led them in a short prayer, and they adjourned the meeting.

Peter took his father aside and said, "Pater, I think you'd better check on some of the new books that have arrived in the library. They're quite different than any we've had there before. At least, they seem different."

"Well, my son, that's always been your job. They keep adding new books every now and then, and they all say about the same things. Just written for different age levels. Is it more 'Peanuts' books?"

"No, sir. These are some that were donated to the library by Mr. Logan and his wife and by the Gordon family."

"Not books on witchcraft?"

"Oh, no."

"Sex books?"

"Oh, dear no, Pater. *Au contraire!*"

"Proverbs says, 'A wise son heareth his father's instruction: but a scorner heareth not rebuke.' "

"And that means?"

"That means, my son, I first have to check out the organ for Timothy who's complaining that some of the stops are stuck, and he can't play the Franck piece he likes. Then I have to repair some of the toys in the nursery. Baby Mary is exceedingly strong for her age. Look over the books yourself, and I'll get around to it what time I may."

Peter took off his glasses, blew on them with his warm cheesey breath, and wiped them carefully on a paper napkin stuck in his pocket for a handkerchief. He was disappointed that his father had declined to look over the books. There was something about them that was very exciting and he longed to share it with someone.

Thursday morning following the mouse conclave, Miriam Maxom, official church secretary, was nervously arranging papers and books in the new minister's office. She and assistant secretary, Patti Barnum, had spent the previous week cleaning out the study and had everything spic and span for the arrival of Dr. Mahoney. The Reverend Mr. Hanagan had been extremely careless and untidy and had left behind a multitude of unfiled and extraneous material. Tom Packney and Mr. Walters had vacuumed, cleaned and painted the study until the smell of turpentine and varnish was overpowering. All the windows were open, and the room was very cold. Miriam stopped to put on a sweater.

She deftly uncorked a bottle of room deodorant and hid it on the window ledge behind the rust-colored curtains. Finally she closed the windows, stepped back to look at the results of her endeavors and thought that probably Dr. Mahoney would be pleased with the tasteful way things were arranged. Mr. Hanagan would never allow her to change or move anything around in the study so the very day he retired she and Patti went to work arranging things to suit themselves.

A tufted gold vinyl couch occupied the wall immediately to the right of the door. Underneath the two ground-floor windows she'd placed a drum table and two black vinyl chairs. Beneath the two windows on the adjacent wall was a tea table upon which stood a silver tea service, a previous gift from the Women's Association to the pastor's study. Not to the pastor, it was understood, but to the study. Two straight-backed chairs with bittersweet velvet cushions flanked the table. The remaining wall was covered with shelves, many reference books and a walk-in closet.

In the center of the room Miriam had instructed Tom Packney to put the pastor's desk and chair. The rich brown, walnut desk top was shined and polished, left completely bare except for a desk calendar and a brown leather letter box. Only one picture was in the room and that was an autumn scene of gold and brown hanging over the couch.

Parts of it were the exact shade of bittersweet as the chair cushions. The trustees had bought an antique gold plush carpet, and the overall effect was that of restrained good looks, tastefully arranged, Miriam decided. She was delighted.

Miriam Maxom, age thirty-six, had been secretary at BPC for twelve years. She'd arrived the same day as the Reverend Mr. Hanagan. Not nearing the age of retirement, she wouldn't dream of leaving, though she often dreamed of other things.

Chiefly, she dreamed of meeting a handsome young man, preferably a minister, a doctor or a lawyer, who'd sweep her off her feet and into a palatial home with three servants and two cars. Being neither beautiful nor gorgeous, she could best be described in the words she had used for the room — restrained good looks, tastefully arranged.

In other words, those of Tom Packney, she just escaped being mousey because of her good-looking figure. Her short wavy hair was the same shade of brown as Jeremiah's daughter Phoebe, and Miriam also had hers frosted occasionally. Her face was plain, eyes nondescript gray, and she tended to dress in the style of a secretary of the 1960's — plain, longish skirts, blouses and tailored suits. Her gray tweed skirt and yellow blouse were topped by a mustard yellow sweater — lovely colors in themselves, but on Miriam they gave her skin a sallow look. She didn't smile often, and that contributed to her plainness. But she was super-efficient, and men can overlook many things in a secretary if she's efficient.

Mice, however, overlook little and can be very outspoken, if only because nobody can hear them. Thus it was that Jeremiah and Priscilla were peeping from a crack in the closet door as Miriam surveyed the room she'd prepared for Dr. Mahoney.

"Can't think why she didn't leave it the way it was when Mr. Hanagan had it," Jeremiah complained to his wife. "I go along with St. Paul when it comes to women being silent in church. And that includeth not moving the furniture!" This earned him a sharp poke in the ribs from Priscilla.

"Excepting thee, my dear, excepting thee," he hastened to assure her. Then both fell to criticizing Miss Maxom's selected color scheme and the vinyl furniture.

"Do you know how hard it is to get a foothold on that slippery stuff? Verily, it's enough to drive a mouse to drink." Priscilla had just opened her mouth to agree when a strange male voice sounded in the very doorway through which Miss Maxom was departing. They heard a sharp cry.

"Oh, I beg your pardon, miss. I'm sorry to have stepped on your toes. I'm the new minister, and I seem to have gotten off on the wrong foot."

Jeremiah groaned at the dreadful pun, but Miss Maxom, unaccustomed as she was to smiling, went into gales of hysterical laughter. This was not the way she'd planned to meet the incoming pastor.

She stammered and blushed and continued to stand in the doorway so that the minister couldn't enter with his bag and two boxes. He set them on the floor in the hallway and removed his hat.

"My name is Andrew Mahoney. You wouldn't be Miss Maxom, would you?"

"Of course I would! I'd love to!" Miss Maxom managed to acknowledge her identity and still occupy the doorway.

In the closet, Jeremiah and Priscilla were "breaking up" as Tom Packney would say. "She's a case, that one," Jeremiah whispered to his wife.

"Do you mind if I bring in these boxes?" the Reverend Doctor Mahoney inquired of his new secretary. At this she turned so abruptly to get out of his way that she tripped over the trustee's new carpet and fell sprawling at his feet. Jeremiah laughed out loud.

Dr. Mahoney put his hat on his bag and gently extricated Miss Maxom's heel from the carpet, setting her on her feet and clearing the way for himself to enter with his belongings. Miss Maxom's sallow cheeks were as red as the new minister's hair, and she was quite unable to speak. Jeremiah continued laughing. Priscilla merely giggled, feeling a little sorry for the secretary.

Turning his head in the direction of the closet Andrew Mahoney asked, "Do you hear something coming from the closet? Is it the heating pipes or what is that high-pitched squeak?" Jeremiah's blood froze as he grabbed Priscilla by the paw and vaulted with her to the shelf above, hiding behind Volume VII–VIII of the Minutes of the Session. Over and over he muttered Proverbs 22:3. "A prudent man foreseeth the evil, and hideth himself; but the simple pass on and are punished."

"Oh, boy," he panted to Priscilla. "We've got one with eyes that seeth and ears that heareth. We're in trouble!"

CHAPTER TWO

Man Is Born to Trouble

MIRIAM MAXOM finally managed to get herself under control and to show Andrew Mahoney around his new study. He dutifully followed her about as she explained where the electrical outlets were, about the tea service and the telephone system. She was most keenly aware of the rugged good looks of this man chosen by the pulpit committee to serve as pastor of Bellview Presbyterian Church. He was tall and well-built, in the manner of traditional college athletes. Curly red hair, deep blue eyes and sand-colored eyebrows she mentally photographed for future reference. He hadn't yet smiled but she was certain his teeth would be straight, white and even. He wore a navy blue topcoat over a pale blue sweater and dark trousers. And wonder of wonders, his black shoes were polished to a high sheen. Mr. Hanagan's black shoes hadn't been polished since the day he arrived at BPC, and they were probably the same shoes he left in, Miriam thought.

Just as they were approaching the walk-in closet, Dr. Mahoney's voice rose above the mouse heartbeats. "I'm sure this will do fine, Miss Maxom. I'll just unpack my books and things, and then I'm to meet your elder Jim Logan for lunch."

"I'll be perfectly happy to unpack for you, Dr. Mahoney," Miriam assured him, anxious for a chance to show that she was in actuality more efficient than it seemed.

"That's all right; I can manage. I'll call you if I need you." He smiled then and her mental camera quickly clicked off the additional details of straight, white, even teeth. "I'll let you know when Mr. Logan arrives," she told him. He smiled again, nodded and removed his overcoat. Instead of putting it in the closet, he threw it on the couch, and the two mice breathed deeply. Safe — for awhile, anyway.

When the mouse family gathered for lunch in the kitchen cabinet, Jeremiah told them of the morning's adventure.

He read one of the Psalms to them, as this was their time for midday worship. The reading of the beautiful words served to quiet everyone, and Jeremiah began to think perhaps they might be safe after all. "We'll abandon our practice of checking out the study daily and concentrate on the Founder's Room and the Music Room. I daresay he won't go in there too often. He doesn't strike me as the musical type."

All the little mice had comments and suggestions to make, most of which boiled down to keeping things status quo. Priscilla served a tasty cheese pie and they all felt much better. Nevertheless, everyone ate with quick, nervous bites; their saucer-like ears turning radar fashion to catch the slightest foreign sound.

In the filing cabinet in Miss Maxom's office, Phoebe stuck her head up for a breath of "uncarbonated" air, just as the secretary returned to her typewriter, still ruffled after her encounter with the new minister. Patti Barnum, petite, blonde and twenty-two, began asking questions.

"What's he like, Miriam? He sure looked handsome when he asked me where his office was. Is he really super?"

"I don't know what you mean, Patti, but he seems nice enough. I can't say if he's super or not." She couldn't help thinking he was a bit clumsy to have stepped on her gray suede shoes.

Patti continued. "I don't think he looks a bit like a minister. Certainly not like Mr. Hanagan or Mr. Norcross of First Baptist. And he's utterly and completely different from Father O'Donnell."

"Who's Father O'Donnell?" Miriam felt she had to ask, though she cared not the slightest.

"Oh, he's the priest at St. Ignatius, where I go. He's old and creaky, but right on!"

Sometimes Miriam had trouble following Patti's conversations and this was one of the times. Phoebe, listening from the upper drawer understood perfectly. Though old and creaky, Father O'Donnell identified with the young folks and understood them. Phoebe and the pharmacy crowd had seen a movie only last week on television that was very much like what Patti described. Sometimes Phoebe got so annoyed with Miss Maxom and her lack of understanding that she chewed minute holes in the carbon paper and thoroughly enjoyed seeing the frustration on the secretary's face when words came out missing. Today Phoebe planned to chew Miss M.'s typewriter eraser off to the nub. That should set her corpuscles racing.

Elder Jim Logan arrived to take the new minister to lunch. He was accompanied by another elder, Harold Bishop. Phoebe got a glimpse of the new man as the three strolled down the hall and out to the parking lot. "Whee-wwee-ooo," Phoebe squeaked. "He is certainly one good-looking seminary biggie." She could hardly wait to tell John Mark that she thought he'd be ultra-liberal and ultra-modern.

When she told this to John Mark, who had also seen him in the hall, John Mark disagreed. "If he were ultra-liberal and mod, he'd have a red beard, longish hair and wear sandals. This time you missed the boat, kiddo. Let's go see what Peter and Timothy think."

All day Saturday people came in and out of the general offices trying to get a look at the new minister. There were those, of course, who knew him already — the members of the nominating committee. Others were merely curious. Some were loyal friends of Mr. Hanagan who hated to see him retire and who were prepared to dislike the new man on sight. Others were sick to death of hearing the same old sermons from Mr. Hanagan and were prepared to welcome the new man with open arms. (Miss Maxom was one of those.)

The director of music, Carlo Entini, had already made his acquaintance and was assured that Dr. Mahoney wouldn't in the least interfere with his plans and selections. Carlo hated to have to tell Dr. Mahoney on his first day that the organ needed repair. But tell him he must. Some of the stops weren't working, and Carlo didn't see how it was possible to play hymns and the anthem on Sunday without those stops. Also, the bombard on had been acting up lately, but those experts the organ company sent out two weeks ago had found nothing wrong. Carlo was extremely frustrated.

When Dr. Mahoney returned from lunch with the two elders, the atmosphere seemed a bit strained, and Dr. Mahoney's face seemed just a trifle pinker than it was when he went out. He asked Miss Maxom to see that he wasn't disturbed. He set about polishing up his first sermon for Bellview Presbyterian Church. Everyone left him alone, even

the mice. They settled down for a short winter's nap in their
weekend retreat — a small burrow near the big oak tree.

Jeremiah, Priscilla and the five young mice were ready for
the eleven o'clock service half an hour early. It was imperative they arrive in time to process to the choir loft before the
choir and the congregation came in, otherwise seven shiny
mice might possibly attract attention. It wouldn't do to miss
the Reverend Doctor Andrew Pinkham Mahoney's first
sermon. They found places along the lattice work which
partially hid the organ pipes from view. There they blended
in nicely with the woodwork and had an excellent view of
choir, minister and congregation, though it was a little
draftier than their usual seats in the balcony.

Jeremiah had brought along his notebook hoping to learn
a few words from the divinity school which were perhaps
newer than those used by Mr. Hanagan. Timothy had his
miniature tape recorder as he dearly loved to tape the organ
prelude and postlude. His favorite Franck piece was being
played today, and he hoped it would help him with his own
lessons. Phoebe had made herself a lavender jumper which
was an exact match of the stencil streaks she habitually wore.

Peter polished his glasses over and over. John Mark
nibbled at a corner of the lattice work while Baby Mary had
her twelve o'clock bottle an hour early. Priscilla believed that
women should have their heads covered in church and so was
wearing a white bonnet which she'd made quite stiff by
dipping in the Elmer's Glue in the kindergarten class room.
One couldn't always get starch these days and one made do
with what was available. Jeremiah's black suit, for instance,
was tailored from a cotton glove found in a supply room
closet.

The congregation was somewhat larger than usual. Out of
a membership of close to a thousand people, usually about

two hundred and fifty to three hundred showed up each Sunday. Today Jeremiah estimated that to be closer to four hundred. Christmas, Easter and a new pastor brought out both the faithful and the unfaithful. Carlo Entini led the congregation in a rousing rendition of "Joyful, Joyful, We Adore Thee." It was probably beautifully done, but Jeremiah and the mouse family soon discovered that it is difficult to hear the words when you are sitting in the music. They resolved not to sit near the organ pipes next Sunday.

Elder Harold Bishop introduced the new minister after the usual reading of the Psalms by the young student assistant from the seminary. Dr. Mahoney acknowledged the gracious introduction with a smile but no speech. When he rose to his full six feet, his red hair shone like a beacon against his black robe and white collar. He read from the fifth chapter of Job.

"For affliction does not come from the dust, nor does trouble sprout from the ground: but man is born to trouble as the sparks fly upward.

"As for me, I would seek God, and to God would I commit my cause; who does great and unsearchable, marvelous things without number."

"That's RSV," murmured Peter, who knew all the versions of the Bible. He adjusted his blue polka dot bow tie.

"Sssh-hh!" commanded his father.

Andrew Mahoney was speaking. He didn't clear his throat as did Mr. Hanagan. He just began to speak in a clear, deep voice.

"I arrived here in Bellview, New Jersey, on Wednesday. Coming as I did from the fairly sheltered life of a professor in a divinity school in the midwest, I was thrilled to see the long line of cars waiting to enter the church parking lot. This, I thought, must be a red-hot church, if people wait in line to get in. Then I discovered that it was merely a shortcut to the nearest gas station, and the people were seeking fuel of a different nature.

"Since then I've seen a remarkable illustration of that part of Job which says, 'man is born to trouble as the sparks fly upward.' Let me tell you a few of the troubles I've been greeted with.

"Your newspaper headlines shriek of gas rationing, oil shortage, energy crunch and rising prices. They speak of Mr. Kissinger pouring oil upon the troubled waters of the Egyptian crisis. Somebody ought to tell him that oil on the water is pollution as well as a waste of energy. But what about local troubles?

"Well, I discover we've got our share of those. The Board of Education is attempting to force a 12 million dollar budget down the throats of the reluctant people of Bellview.

"And, I've been told, there's even trouble in Bellview Presbyterian Church. The organ refuses to behave correctly, and membership has fallen off. You haven't met the proposed budget in six years, and repairs are overdue to the church building. There's division within the ranks of the church, and no strong youth leadership. As for myself, there's a high-pitched squeak somewhere in my office that I'm unable to find, and it's driving me nuts!"

The congregation gave a nervous laugh, so relieved were they to have done with the catalog of woes. Jeremiah gave a nervous twitch.

Dr. Mahoncy flipped a page in his black notebook and smiled.

"Don't get the idea that I've come to correct all these misfortunes. Some of them are clearly out of my territory. By the time I've reorganized and changed a few things, called for more meetings instead of fewer, asked for more leadership and more pledges, you'll probably be ready to send me back." Nervous laughter again. The mice were pinching each other and making remarks most uncomplimentary to Dr. Mahoney. Only Peter was silent and Baby Mary, whose bottle was just about to go empty.

Then it seemed that he would redeem himself in all eyes for he quoted again, "As for me, I would seek God, and to God would I commit my cause; who does great things and unsearchable things without number."

Yes, they began to relax in the pews as he concluded that God would be able to handle everything with only a little cooperation from them. Really, they hadn't minded the verbal spanking too much, as long as he stroked their heads at the finish. Yes, and maybe we needed a good shaking-up, some of them thought. Maybe we need some new blood in the pulpit.

Mr. Hanagan's Loyals, however, were raging inside. Mr. Hanagan never talked to them like that. He never preached from the newspaper. He only preached the gospel and quoted from the Lord Jesus Christ — never from Henry Kissinger!

There was a division in the church, all right, and the Reverend Dr. Mahoney had just widened it with his own little trowel. Ah, too bad, but it did seem that sparks might fly not only upward but in all directions. The announced meeting of the session for the following Wednesday night was tantamount to a flung gauntlet.

"Oh, boy," said Jeremiah to Priscilla. "Verily, he should have spared the rod on the first Sunday, anyway. I'm afraid that red hair bodes ill for somebody."

CHAPTER THREE

The First Epistle of Andrew to the Session

WEDNESDAYS SEEMED fated to be important days in the life of the new minister. He had arrived at BPC on the Wednesday previous. This Wednesday he was preparing the agenda for his first session meeting. It was also his first introduction to Tom Packney, seventeen-year-old assistant custodian. Tom, who usually worked at BPC after school and on weekends had been on a short vacation, visiting colleges, one of which he hoped to attend next year.

At 3:08 p.m. he entered the parking lot at the church, raced the motor of his orange, souped-up, mag-wheeled Volkswagen and loped into the downstairs complex of offices. Tom was lanky, even gangly, and in order to keep from getting his feet tangled up with each other, he customarily loped. It was when he slowed down that he had trouble.

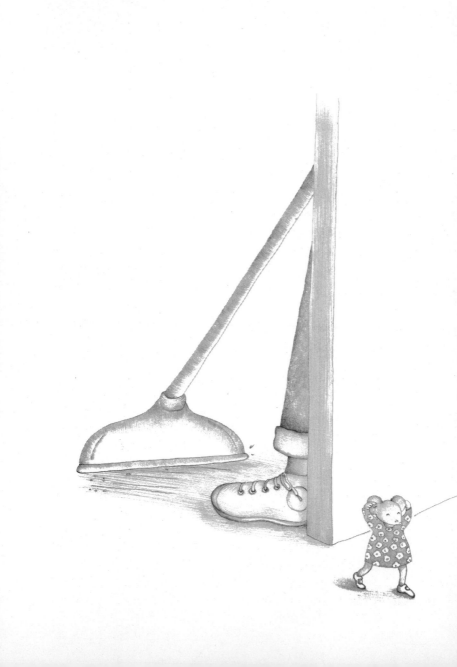

Tom had this thing about pushing the janitor's broom: he couldn't do it. Not without his long legs getting in the way, so Mr. Walters allowed him to vacuum everything. It didn't matter to Mr. Walters, he was almost deaf and the noise was no more to him than the whir of an electric can opener.

It mattered little to Miriam Maxom and Patti Barnum whose electric typewriters, mimeograph machines and telephones gave as good as they got where noise was concerned. It mattered not at all to Carlo Entini, who when he wasn't practicing the organ, was giving piano lessons or directing a choir rehearsal.

But the noise pollution was a severe trial to the Mouse family who loved peace and quiet. When Tom vacuumed the secretary's office, the noise reverberated in Phoebe's filing cabinet until she thought her eardrums would burst. In the library Peter stuffed cotton in his ears and chewed gum, as the noise could easily be compared to the take-off or landing of a 747, and he suffered the same symptoms of ear-popping.

Timothy adopted a so-what attitude. He was so tuned into the pipe organ as to hardly even hear anything else. In the nursery, Baby Mary got scared and ran to find John Mark each time Tom came in to clean. Jeremiah and Priscilla, though belonging to the social house mouse family, the genus *Mus musculus,* preferred the quiet mustiness of religious quarters. They moved from room to room, from office to office, in advance of Tom Packney, trying to guess where he'd go next and keep ahead of him.

"Verily, I feel like a voice crying in the wilderness," quoth Jeremiah. "Prepare ye the way of the vacuum cleaner!"

Today Tom started cleaning the red carpet in the sanctuary, and by 3:38 p.m. he had worked his way downstairs to the uncarpeted hall approaching the minister's study. As he vacuumed he sang rather loudly and quite off-key, "When the Saints Go Marching In."

He had made three passes at the floor in front of Andrew's office, when that gentleman opened the door and stood like a giant squarely within it. It startled Tom, and he let go of the upright sweeper which promptly took off on its own and headed for Andrew's legs.

In a voice so clear and deep that it could be distinctly heard above the machine, Andrew said, "Shut that thing off!"

Tom Packney went pale under his freckles and made a frantic grab at the machine, catching it just as it nudged the polished toes of Dr. Mahoney's black shoes. He flipped the switch to OFF and stood waiting to be executed.

Then, unaccountably, Andrew Mahoney smiled, and for Tom he became in that moment the Pope. It was all he could do to refrain from kissing the ring Andrew wore from Wedgewood Divinity School.

Tom stammered an apology. "Gee, I'm sorry I made so much noise out here. Guess I kinda forgot you'd be in that office."

"Well, Tom — you are Tom, aren't you? Why don't we have an arrangement that if my door is closed you won't vacuum the hall. If it's open you can sweep to your heart's content. It so happens I'm working right now and would appreciate the quiet."

"You bet! I guarantee nobody's gonna run this thing when you're working in your study."

Tom brushed his long sandy hair out of his eyes, gave a military salute in the minister's direction and called out, "It's nice to have you aboard, sir!" He unplugged the sweeper and silently pushed off to greener pastures. Andrew Mahoney had made a friend, and Tom Packney had found a hero.

Miss Maxom rang Dr. Mahoney's office to see if he were ready to have his agenda typed.

"No, it can't be typed, Miss Maxom, because I don't yet know what I'm going to say."

"But it's almost four o' — "

"Yes, I know what time it is, so perhaps I'll just have to work from my notes tonight without a formal agenda."

"You may find it a little difficult," Miriam suggested. "It would be easier if you had copies typed up for the session members to refer to. It's customary, you know."

"Then we'll have to depart from custom and play it by ear." He thanked her again and was still hard at work when he heard her heels clatter down the hall to the side exit. Soon there was no one around but Andrew Mahoney and the mice.

Priscilla was preparing a salmon casserole in the kitchen, and the smell of the creamy concoction wafted ever so gently under the minister's door. It reminded him that he was hungry so he took his notes across the street and sat scribbling at a table in the small delicatessen where he ordered a hot roast beef sandwich. It was then that he wondered who was cooking salmon in the church kitchen. He decided to have a look as he went back to his study.

By the time he finished his meal, the mice had also finished theirs and so he forgot about investigating the kitchen. Eight o'clock found him waiting to greet the ruling elders who comprised the session of Bellview Presbyterian Church. He turned on the lights in the blue-carpeted lounge and took a seat at the small desk there. He rose as the first ones entered, and introduced himself. Some of them he already knew.

Andrew Mahoney called the session meeting to order, and after a short devotional period he proceeded down the line to enumerate the items he proposed that the men and women consider. Number four was the matter of housing.

"Ladies and gentlemen, I'm afraid I'm a little cramped in the small apartment you secured for me and I wonder if the manse will soon be ready for occupancy?" They had agreed to paint some of the rooms before he moved in.

One of the elders spoke up. Andrew thought his name was Gerald Watkins.

"Dr. Mahoney, the work is proceeding slowly on redecorating the manse, mainly because we've been doing it with volunteer labor. Also we wondered if since you're a single man it mightn't be cheaper to let you remain in the apartment and rent out the manse to a family. That is, until such time as you become a family man yourself."

Everyone laughed except Andrew. His reply was clear and concise.

"Mr. Watkins, I'd appreciate it if you'd advise your committee that I plan to move into the manse next week, whether or not it's redecorated. I have many books and belongings, also some furniture of my own which is now in storage. I simply don't choose to live in a tiny apartment just because it would be cheaper. I'm afraid that brings us to the matter of the budget."

The budget was discussed. How were they planning to meet their commitments to the presbytery, synod and mission projects when the pledges obviously were not being met? None of the committees seemed to know.

In his straightforward manner, Andrew asked the session members, "What is wrong with this church? What's happened that causes its members to leave? I've checked the records carefully, and they don't all die or transfer out of town. Most of them stop coming altogether or find other church affiliations within the community. What's wrong with this church?"

Bill Gordon and Jim Logan exchanged glances. Bill Gordon spoke.

"Dr. Mahoney, you've asked a loaded question. I can't speak for everyone here but it's my opinion that this church hasn't really been alive for some time. It must be admitted that the Reverend Hanagan was ultra-conservative, ailing and rather dull. There just hasn't been anything for the people to get excited about. What it really needs is a good shot in the arm."

Gerald Watkins was speaking again. "On the other hand, my family transferred here from the Presbyterian church across town three years ago because we found them to be too liberal. They've taken the general direction that the church as a whole has followed. That is, liberality and social action. Give me conservatism every time."

Muriel Aldamann held up her hand for attention. Dr. Mahoney nodded. "What's really needed here, and what we hope you'll supply, is a middle-of-the-road policy. Nobody really wants extremism in either form." Several women nodded agreement.

Jim Logan, sitting very quietly in a corner, spoke up. "I believe the shot in the arm that Bill is referring to means giving the people something they can commit themselves to. A return to the faith and belief of the New Testament churches. An infusion of God's Holy Spirit to empower our people to change their lives and rededicate themselves to Christ and His service. It's about time we stopped believing in something and started believing in Someone. And that Someone is none other than Jesus Christ, Son of God. When we can really affirm that, then we won't need to ask for more helpers or more pledges. They will automatically follow."

"Very interesting, Mr. Logan," Dr. Mahoney answered

him. "But just how do we go about getting the people to believe in Christ? I suspect most of them do, or they wouldn't be on the church rolls."

"What I mean, I guess," said Jim Logan, "is that God doesn't seem real to most people. When they know Him personally, they'll want to serve Him, no matter what kind of church they're in."

The members were getting restless. It was after eleven, and most of them had heard Jim's belief before. It was something he'd been harping on for several months, close to a year, in fact. Real? Of course God was real. Didn't they affirm this every Sunday in the Apostle's Creed? What on earth was Logan trying to do, stir up trouble?

Dr. Mahoney glanced at his agenda and saw that it couldn't possibly be covered in this meeting, so he set a date for a special meeting one week hence. Then he asked Jim Logan to dismiss the gathering.

"Holy Father, we thank you and praise you for being a God of love and mercy. We thank you for your Son, our Savior and for your Holy Spirit, our Sustainer. In this new year, O Lord, we pray that you will pour out your blessings upon this session, upon this pastor and upon this congregation so that we may serve you more fully and glorify your Son, Jesus. In His name we pray. Amen."

"Amen," said Jeremiah. "That was some prayer, eh?"

From under the couch in the corner, Jeremiah and Peter retreated further into the shadow as the members rose to leave.

"Pater, these men and women could learn something from him; he's got it together, I think. We may yet see *mirabilia* in this place."

"Peter, these people are elders, and they don't talk like that. What do you mean?"

"Wonders and miracles, Pater. Wonders and miracles! By

the way, do you want to look over those books I told you about?"

"Not tonight, son, it's late, and I promised your mother I'd come straight home from the meeting. Maybe tomorrow."

"Well, I think I shall read a little more before I turn in," said Peter. His voice was casual, but he was excited throughout. For the first time in his entire life at BPC, he felt a burning desire to read not just for the learning but for the result of that learning. He could hardly wait to see how the book ended. He picked up his copy of The Living Bible to use in the references. Mr. Gordon's right, he thought. The Living Bible is being read by a dead church. They might need more than an infusion. They might need a complete transfusion!

It was 9:30 on the morning after Andrew Mahoney's first meeting with his session. Miriam Maxom had received several telephone calls from elder Harold Bishop trying to line-up volunteers to finish painting the manse. Each time she gave him a list of names, he exhausted those shortly and called for more. So far only one person had volunteered to help with the last two rooms. He'd started making calls as early as seven a.m., before the commuters left for work. He was now calling a list of unemployed housewives who had no small children, supposedly a good resource. Results zero.

The last time he called, Miriam told him, "You go on to work, Mr. Bishop, and I'll make some calls myself or try to snag someone who comes in today." With a sigh of relief, Harold Bishop hung up, and Miriam returned to her typing.

The light on her desk flickered to indicate that Dr. Mahoney was ready to give dictation. Still flustered by her unfortunate first encounter with the new minister, Miriam had abandoned all hope of changing her initials from the delightful coincidence of M. M. to that of 3-M: Miriam

Maxom Mahoney. No, it hardly seemed likely that she'd ever be able to do more than mumble and stumble around him.

She knocked softly at the minister's door and entered when he called out, "Come in, Miss Maxom."

She expected him to be uptight after his first session meeting but he seemed quite relaxed. He wore a black suit and his clerical collar, expecting to make hospital calls later in the day. Miriam was wearing an oatmeal tweed skirt and a gray silk blouse. Tom Packney often referred to it as her "mouse blouse," but not in her hearing. The mice heard and never quite forgave him.

Jeremiah, who was a dignified shade of gray, felt terribly offended each time she wore it. Priscilla, a dignified shade of brown, didn't much care. She waited with him now in the minister's closet. They felt safer on the fourth shelf and so had made a small but comfortable nest out of a shredded copy of last year's BPC financial report. There were always extra copies of those left over. They were having a midmorning snack of cheese and crackers when the minister began his dictation.

It was his Sunday sermon, full-blown and ready on Thursday morning. Taking as his text, Ecclesiastes 3:1–8, he titled his sermon, "A Season for All Men."

"For everything there is a season and a time for every matter under heaven. A time to be born and a time to die; a time to plant and a time to pluck up what is planted; a time to kill and a time to heal; a time to break down and a time to build up; a time to weep, and a time to laugh; a time to mourn, and a time to dance; a time to cast away stones, and a time to gather stones together; a time to embrace and a time to refrain from embracing; a time to seek, and a time to lose; a time to keep, and a time to cast away; a time to rend, and a time to sew; a time to keep silence, and a time to speak; a

time to love, and a time to hate; a time for war, and a time
for peace."

Upon these verses and several clinical statistics and
editorials he built a sermon on abortion. Miriam blushed at
some of the expressions he used. Jeremiah was livid under his
gray complexion as he and Priscilla listened to the minister's
liberal views.

Jeremiah could also quote from Ecclesiastes and did so,
but louder than he planned. From chapter ten, verse thirteen
he proclaimed: "The beginning of the words of his mouth is
foolishness and the end of his talk is wicked madness."
Priscilla squeezed his paw to let him know that she agreed
with him.

Andrew stopped dictating. "What did you say, Miss
Maxom?"

"Why, nothing, Dr. Mahoney. I said nothing."

"I could have sworn I heard you say that my words are
foolishness and my talk wicked madness."

"Oh, no sir, I never said that. I never said anything!"

Miriam was shaking under her "mouse blouse," but she
remained with pencil poised as Dr. Mahoney rose and
walked around the room. He looked behind the autumnal
picture on the wall. He peered inside the silver teapot. He
opened the closet door and glanced inside.

"Is it possible this room is bugged?" he asked her.

"I keep hearing voices and noises, and I can't seem to find
out where they're coming from."

"Dr. Mahoney, I can assure you this office isn't bugged.
I'm absolutely certain of that." Miriam was vehement in her
denial. Who did he suspect? Herself? One of the elders? The
neighboring Baptist minister?

"Then we must have mice," Andrew declared. "I'll get
some traps tomorrow."

He finished dictating the sermon and asked the secretary to type it and have mimeographed copies made. He thought a number of people might desire copies. As it turned out he was so right.

Miriam had just finished mimeographing the sermon when Tom Packney loped into her office. For a moment she wasn't sure he could apply his brakes before crashing into the machine. She wasn't exactly in a mood to be tolerant.

"Tom, for goodness sake, why do you move so fast? Slow down. You make me nervous."

"Sorry, Miss M. Didn't mean to. Is the Padre around?"

"He's in his office, Tom, but you'd better not clean in there right now. Besides, you're two hours early."

"Oh, I didn't come to work, Miss M. This is my lunch hour. I just came over to see if my buddy, Ted Hinkel, and me could help paint the manse after school and tonight. Turns out we don't have band practice after all."

Tom wasn't prepared for Miss Maxom's reaction. She grabbed him and gave him a big hug and a kiss on the cheek.

"Oh, Tom, what luck! You really are the greatest. Mr. Bishop tried all morning to get someone to help finish the painting and only one person offered to help. With the three of you working I'll bet you can finish up tonight!"

Tom was blushing and wiping at his cheek where Miriam had bussed him. Maybe she wasn't such a "mouse" after all. She buzzed back to ask if Andrew could see Tom for a minute. She nodded to Tom to go in and shortly thereafter Tom was telling his hero of his intentions to finish off the painting.

"Thanks, Tom, that will be just fine. I believe the paint is already in the rooms. Blue in the bedroom and beige in the study. They've left all the equipment out; just get a key from Mr. Walters and start when you're ready. Maybe I might come over and give you a hand myself later on. That be okay?"

"Sure, Padre, we'd like that. We can rap while we paint." Tom was delighted at the prospect. He stood first on one foot and then the other wondering how to make his exit.

"What did you call me, Tom?"

"Oh, gosh, Padre. I didn't mean to call you Padre. I meant to say Dr. Mahoney. It's just that, well — that's the way I think of you when I happen to think of you. As, uh, Padre. But from now on I'll be very careful to say Dr. Mahoney. You know how us teen-agers are!" He laughed to cover a moment of exquisite embarrassment.

Sitting at his desk, Andrew swiveled about in his chair and laid his hand on Tom's arm. "Tom, I'd like to have you call me Padre. That's really nice."

Tom knew how to exit now — smiling, with a farewell wave to his hero. He would have genuflected if he'd known how. Wow, what a swell guy, he thought to himself. What a swell guy!

On his way out, Tom stopped off at Miriam's office to get a key. Mr. Walters was out to lunch, and he knew he could find one here. He picked up one of the minister's sermons. "Okay if I take this to read during independent study?"

"Sure, Tom, help yourself." Miriam would have given him the key to the vault, if he'd asked for it at that moment, so glad was she to be able to report to Mr. Bishop that his problem was solved. At this rate, Dr. Mahoney could be moved into the manse by Saturday. Miriam planned to offer to help decorate and arrange the furniture. She didn't know that the Women's Association had already set themselves that task.

When Patti Barnum came back from lunch, Miriam went to the neighboring delicatessen for a salad and tea. Suddenly remembering the content of the sermon she had put into the hands of gullible Tom Packney, she felt a moment of panic. Heaven only knew how he would interpret the Reverend Dr. Mahoney's stance on abortion.

Tom was even then interpreting it to some of his friends who joined him in the school lounge for independent study. "Independent study" for this particular group of students consisted of drinking Cokes and smoking cigarettes. A few students came in just to sit and relax. A poker game had started up in one corner of the lounge. Very soon Tom had a larger audience than the poker players, as he read and commented on the minister's sermon.

One interested listener was the editor of the school paper, *The Bell Tower*. Bibs Hanlon, a short blonde senior, with an eye on a journalism scholarship, asked if she might borrow it until fifth period.

"Sure," Tom said. "You can come and hear it Sunday if you want to. Why don't you?" To Tom this was the best idea since open-lunch was declared legal. He'd had his eye on Bibs all last year, but Elizabeth Hanlon had never, until this minute, given him the time of day.

"Maybe I will, Tom. I'll call you."

Tom floated off to Spanish class; for once his feet tracked side by side without getting entangled. He dreamed of himself and Bibs kneeling before an altar while the Padre performed a marriage ceremony. "Muy bonita, muy bonita," he said over and over to himself.

What Jeremiah was saying to himself and to his assembled family who dallied over a late lunch of spiced ham and cheese was an altogether different story.

"It's an ill wind that bloweth in yon hallowed halls. Confound it, why can't he stick to Biblical subjects?"

He was just about to expound on the coming attraction when Priscilla caught his eye. "Jeremiah dear, there are little ears present. Could we postpone this discussion until nap-time?"

Jeremiah agreed and hurriedly rushed Baby Mary off to her nap and John Mark off to play. He was about to dispatch Phoebe to the Pharmacy to visit her friends when she protested.

"Father, I'm old enough to listen to this sermon if Peter and Timothy are. You forget I'm vice-president of our chapter of Mouse Libbers and we frequently have speakers who lecture on the subject of abortion, equal rights and other neat topics."

Jeremiah opened his mouth to answer, just as one of his closest friends, Reginald Rat from the Hardware Store, walked in. Reggie, rugged Reggie, liked to think of himself as educated and would speak extemporaneously on any given subject. Jeremiah knew for a fact that Reginald had scarcely gone beyond the seed catalogs that littered the back room of the Hardware Store. True, he had given his friend a copy of King James Version of the Bible, but the last time Jeremiah saw it in use was three years ago when Reggie, in a fit of spring cleaning, threw a cloth over it and put a can of dandelions on top. "For that feminine touch every room needs," said Reginald.

How can we discuss this in front of Reggie, Jeremiah wondered. He needn't have; the moment greetings were over, Timothy held up his hand and without waiting for permission, lapsed into a lengthy defense of the forthcoming sermon.

"It's about time man started to face up to the problems of over-population and pollution. I like this man's views on abortion. It makes sense to me. Let the circumstances dictate the decision. The Bible says there's a time to be born and a time to die. If a woman decides not to have a baby due to mitigating circumstances, I say that's legal and moral and her own business. In fact — "

Peter interrupted. "Your exegesis leaves something to be desired, brother Timothy. You are overlooking the Biblical injunction, 'Thou shalt not kill.' "

Jeremiah quickly stepped into the breach. "Peter, I don't like to hear you take the name of the Lord in vain. In future kindly refrain from using the expression 'eggsy-Jesus.' "

Priscilla busied herself with tidying up the lunch things. This sort of talk was most embarrassing to her. Not at all like when she was a girl, living modestly in the cathedral in Newark. And she had tried so hard to bring up the children to be obedient, gently-bred and well-mannered. And here was Peter using slang words in the same breath as the name of the dear Lord Jesus.

Reginald Rat could stand the suspense no longer.

"What in the all-fired tarnation are you all so het up about?"

Jeremiah then had to explain. Reginald hadn't yet met the new minister, and Jeremiah hoped to keep it that way. There was hardly any way to disguise a rat the size of Reggie. He'd be sure to stand out in a crowd.

So to placate his old friend, Jeremiah brought him up-to-date on all the happenings since Andrew Mahoney's arrival. He leaned heavily on the Reverend's liberal interpretation of the Scriptures and his penchant for preaching from the headlines of the morning paper or the eleven o'clock news. Reginald was aware of Jeremiah's faithful adherence to the Bible's literal meaning and of his deep devotion to its commandments. Contrary to what Jeremiah thought, Reginald had read the Bible through many times.

But Reginald, hairy and uncouth of manner, was a rat's rat at heart. If a mess could be made he made it. Deliberately he refused to use the deodorant sprays well-meaning friends gave him at Christmas. His sloppy, odorous and cluttered penthouse apartment in a storage barrel was heaven to him. He was by nature truculent, argumentative and aggravating. He also knew it irritated Jeremiah greatly to have the Biblical concepts questioned, altered or changed. He proceeded, therefore, to shock the pants off his oldest and dearest friend, Jeremiah Malachi Mouse.

CHAPTER FOUR

Head Winds

THE MOUSE family were lunching in a warm, secluded corner of a storage cabinet in the church kitchen, near the stove. The pilot light kept the interior of the stove warm, and the stove connected to the cabinet, and the cabinet connected to the cracker boxes and the dried soup boxes and the Lipton Tea boxes. Priscilla had set a clean white cloth on a large cracker box from which they ate. They, Jeremiah, Peter and Timothy were sitting erect on tea boxes and toothpick cartons. Reginald, seated on a raisin package, helped himself to a sardine, leaned back against the cabinet wall and put his feet on the table. Then he began to pick his teeth with a toothpick that protruded from the box on which young Timothy sat.

Jeremiah was disgusted. He does it deliberately to annoy me, he thought. Sometimes friends can be a trial. He'd no idea just how much of a trial Reginald had set out to be. Reginald began to speak, removing the toothpick occasionally to puff on it in the manner of Sir Winston Churchill with his elegant cigar. Phoebe asked to be excused, and Priscilla left to do the laundry in the kitchen sink above them.

"My friend," Reginald looked at Jeremiah, ignoring the two younger mice. "My friend, you and your Bible! Don't you know that book's out-of-date and completely irrelevant to today's world? Who lives according to them statues, anyway?"

This is not to be borne, thought Peter. "Don't you mean statutes, Brother Rat?"

"Statutes, schmatutes, whatever; the thing's old-fashioned. And it's discriminatin' to boot. I give you Leviticus 11:29 where the Lord told Moses and Aaron, 'these are unclean to you: the weasel, the mouse and the great lizard.' Unclean, mind you; He declared us unclean!"

Peter retorted. "But that was so they wouldn't be eaten. If it weren't for that verse you might well be on the menu at the delicatessen today!"

Jeremiah raised his voice, confronting Reginald directly. "I'll see your Leviticus 11:29 and raise you I Samuel 6:4,5 and 18."

"Pater!" a shocked Peter exclaimed.

"Attaboy, Pop," Timothy exulted.

Jeremiah was off and running. "After the Philistines had captured the Ark of the Covenant and had kept it for seven months, they desired to return it, so they called the priests and diviners together and asked how they could go about it. The priests told them to hitch two unused milk cows to a cart and put the Ark inside the cart. *But,* they were not to return it alone. No, they were to send along five golden mice as a guilt offering to the Lord. *Five golden mice!*"

"And a partridge in a pear tree," was Reginald's tuneful rejoinder. "And if I remember my I Samuel, I recall they were also told to send along five golden tumors. Somehow, it don't thrill me to be put in the same class as a tumor." Reginald could tell by his friend's expression that he'd trumped Jeremiah's face card. He decided to go for broke.

"And my dear friend, Jeremiah. How is it that the Lord takes care of the lilies and the sparrows (them lousy sparrows!) but does he take care of the mice? Forget it! We're persecuted, trapped, snapped and slapped. Poisoned, hounded, with our tails cut off by a farmer's wife, wielding a great big carving knife. They were blind already; you think she'd be satisfied with a blind mouse, but no — she hadda have 'em tailless."

"That's not the Bible, and it's not God who persecutes us, it's men," said Peter, who'd just about had it with this discussion. "You had better believe that if he didn't have the whole world in his hand, you wouldn't take another breath. He cares for every living thing. I think it was George Macdonald who posited that the Lord cared more for a lowly oxen than he did for the most magnificent star in the heavens.

"Brother Rat, and I call you that in the truest sense of the word, as I believe we are all brothers in God's sight, it behooves you to praise God for all things! Not just for your daily cheese but for that sciatic leg you drag around and the drafty home you've made in the Hardware Store, because it's praise that releases the power through which God works. Praise the Lord!"

Reginald stopped picking his teeth. Jeremiah sat open-mouthed, and Timothy fell off the toothpick box.

"Wherever did you get all that?" his father asked.

"In those new books you've been so reluctant to look into. And there's lots more where that came from and it's all in the Bible! I looked it up." With that he stood up and delivered his final salvo. "All of you had better rid yourselves of your *parti pris*, your preconceived opinions, and get with it, for the time of *koinonia* is at hand. Praise the Lord, I say, and praise Him again!"

Andrew Mahoney stepped into the kitchen in time to hear the final salvo. He'd come in to make himself a cup of tea. He withdrew his hand from the teakettle as though it were a flaming sword and made his way hurriedly back to the office.

"It's not mice, it's my head! I've got to have it examined."

He burst in so unexpectedly upon Miriam Maxom that she was startled into insensibility. He came through the swinging door from the outer hall just as she was leaving by that route to post some letters. Being the bigger of the two, his entrance sent the poor secretary flying, and she landed against the wall, scattering letters all over the floor. She couldn't remain leaning against the wall because she was breathless and so slumped to the floor at his feet.

"Quick, Miss Barnum, call a doctor and make an appointment."

"For Miss Maxom?"

"No, for me! It's my head!"

Fifteen minutes later, Andrew sat wrapped in a sheet on the edge of an examining table in the office of Dr. Abernathy. The doctor's sole recommendation, as far as the minister was concerned, was that he was only one block away from church and happened to have had a cancellation.

"When did you first begin to hear these voices?" asked the bearded Dr. Abernathy.

"Only since I came to the Bellview Church. What do you think it is, doctor?"

The doctor took his time about answering. He was overweight, moved rather slowly and thought accordingly. He liked to make sound decisions. With Andrew's chart before him, he scanned it carefully.

"Get dressed, Dr. Mahoney, and come into my office."

Failure to get an answer convinced Andrew that Dr. Abernathy had stumbled onto a disease so virulent that it couldn't be mentioned. Andrew put his socks on wrong side out, and forgot to zip his trousers.

"I think you left something undone," said Dr. Abernathy, glancing at Andrew's slacks. Andrew quickly zipped and waited expectantly for the doctor's diagnosis.

Dr. Abernathy again went through the figures and notations he'd made on a five-by-eight white card. Finally he spoke.

"Dr. Mahoney, I can find absolutely nothing wrong with you. You are in perfect physical health. In fact, you look like you might be playing for the Miami Dolphins."

"But the voices?"

"I think it's possible that you are a little nervous about being in a new church and perhaps have a few too many problems. Your EKG is excellent and so is your electroencephalogram. Blood pressure is perfect; heart and lungs normal, splendid muscle tone. Not even enlarged tonsils."

"I had those out when I was five."

"Have you checked into the heating system in the church? Sometimes radiators make a hissing noise. Or the wind. Or mice — you might be hearing mice. At any rate, I'm going to give you a prescription for a tranquilizer. Try taking one of these at bedtime and during the day if you feel you're getting upset or hearing voices. Usually when one hears voices it's accompanied by a ringing in the ears as well, and that might denote hardening of the arteries. But I can safely say, you have the arteries of a thirty-year-old man."

"I'm only thirty-two," said Andrew, feeling not too comforted.

The doctor scribbled something on a prescription pad. "Stop at the pharmacy and have this filled and I think you'll find that the voices go away. If, however," and he paused, rose from his chair and looked out the window toward Linwood Avenue, "if they should continue or other symptoms develop, then I recommend that you see a psychiatrist. It could mean something serious."

Andrew found it hard to walk after having the rug pulled from under his feet. He put on his coat, told the nurse to send him a bill and stopped in the pharmacy to have his prescription filled. He didn't know that Phoebe was right at his feet, visiting under the cashier's counter with Elma Evelyn Kathleen McMouse, who lived in an old Kleenex box.

Phoebe perked up her frosted little ears when she heard the minister's voice. "That's our new minister. I think he's kinda nutty. Wonder why he needs medicine? Wanta come hear him Sunday? He's gonna preach on abortion."

Elma Evelyn Kathleen allowed as how she would and then remarked, "Maybe your nut is cracking up!"

Andrew heard every syllable. He turned so pale that the pharmacist hurried with his prescription, hoping that he mightn't pass out while waiting.

Pocketing his bottle of capsules, Andrew went next door to the hardware store.

"I'd like four dozen mousetraps. The biggest you've got."

Mr. Wheeler discovered that he only had three dozen. Andrew took those, ordered another dozen to be delivered to the church.

"You mean the Baptist Church on the corner?"

"Certainly not, I mean the Presbyterian Church across the street."

He made a strange sight going out the back door of the hardware store, with flaming red hair, a sky blue windbreaker with BHS BAND on the back, clerical collar and a clear plastic bag full of thirty-six mousetraps. He had grabbed Tom Packney's jacket in his haste to reach the doctor.

Unknown to Andrew Mahoney, Reginald Rat had his first glimpse of him as he exited through Reginald's bailiwick. Peeping through a hole in a huge brown barrel, Reginald saw the six-foot, redheaded, mousetrapped minister. As fast as his sciatica would allow, Reggie hotfooted it back to BPC to spread the alarm.

"They'll see I was right about persecution," he muttered to himself. "Let's see if the Lord can save them from the traps."

Jeremiah took the news calmly and called his family together for a council. Within thirty minutes they'd formulated a plan to seek and destroy all traps as found.

Gathered around an old shoe in the janitor's closet, with Jeremiah sitting on the tongue, they finished their preparations and Peter was asked to dismiss them.

"Praise God from whom all blessings flow! Praise Him all creatures here below. Praise Him with a thousand tongues; Praise Him with our heavenly songs. We praise you, and thank you, Father, for even this our persecution. We know that all things work together so that your will might be done. Even so, Lord Jesus, we lift you up and glorify your name and ask that you keep us all in safety. Amen."

Priscilla thought she had never heard a more beautiful prayer. Peter was so changed lately. So much more loveable.

Reginald thought Peter was going to preach. Ask for a prayer, and you get a sermon. That's what comes of allowing young folks to get so much learning.

Jeremiah for once was speechless. He barely managed an audible, "Amen."

Back at the church Andrew found no one around who might set out the mousetraps and bait them, so he dumped them in a corner of his office. Mr. Walters was not to be seen, and he remembered that Tom would be painting at the

manse. It was almost six o'clock anyway, and the secretaries had gone.

On impulse, Andrew stopped at the local pizzeria. He ordered a large sausage pizza and four Cokes which he took to the manse. Tom and his friend Ted had been painting for two hours while the third man, Jack Kimberley, had arrived shortly after. They all enjoyed a pizza break, sitting on the floor in the kitchen. Andrew borrowed a pair of old coveralls which Kimberley had in the back of his car. He likewise returned Tom Packney's jacket.

"Hey, I wondered where I left that."

Andrew didn't tell him that he'd worn it by mistake. Somehow the occasion didn't seem right. He and Tom painted the study while Ted and Jack Kimberley finished off the bedroom. Andrew anticipated moving in on Saturday.

It had been a long time since Andrew had wielded a paint brush, but he found that it was quite relaxing, and he enjoyed it. To keep his black shoes from getting paint-spattered, he painted in his sock feet. Being black, it wasn't easy to tell that they were on the wrong side out, except that they felt itchier. It had been a long day, and Andrew would gladly have been silent, but Tom had other ideas.

"You know that sermon you're gonna do on abortion?" Tom flailed away at the wall from atop a five-foot ladder. "Wow, it really made a hit at school today!"

Andrew, at the adjoining wall, almost tripped over his paint bucket in surprise. "At *school*? How did my sermon get to school?"

"Oh, Miss Maximum let me have a copy when I stopped in at lunch."

"Miss Maximum? Do you mean Miss Maxom?"

"Oh, yeah — Miss Maxom. But sometimes I kid her and call her Miss Maximum. She kinda likes it."

"I imagine," said Andrew. "But getting back to my

sermon, don't you think it was a bit presumptuous to distribute it before I even delivered it?"

"Well, maybe, but I can guarantee you're gonna have a crowd from BHS there to hear it. Abortion and the new morality are big issues right now. You should hear some of the kids discuss it in sex ed. They thought your sermon was right on."

Andrew began to feel itchy all over, and a vague feeling of uneasiness settled over him. He barely heard Tom's remark about Bibs Hanlon planning to cover the sermon for the school paper, and that the sex ed teacher would like to meet him. Loud and clear, he heard him say that Mr. and Mrs. Packney were very irritated at the subject he had chosen.

He began to feel so uneasy that he decided perhaps the pizza hadn't agreed with him, so he stopped to take a tranquilizer. Fifteen minutes later he fell asleep while squatting to paint the bottom of the wall under the window.

Tom looked down just as the minister's head slumped between his knees and the paint brush fell to the floor.

"Gosh, Padre, you really must be tired. Why don't you go on home, and we'll finish up here. Haven't got much more to do." Andrew didn't answer. He was sound asleep, squatting Indian fashion on the floor.

Taking matters into his own hands, Tom called out to Jack Kimberley.

"Hey, Mr. Kimberley, come here a second, will you?"

"What happened, Tom?"

"Guess his Reverence isn't used to painting or maybe he's allergic or something. Anyway, he's asleep. Really zonked out. How about if I take him home and then come back and finish up?"

"Okay, Tom, I'll help you get him in the car, but he's in no shape to drive. Why don't you drive his Chevy, and I'll follow you in my car and bring you back?"

Supported by two of his parishioners, Andrew made it to his apartment. Tom and Mr. Kimberley zipped off the paint-stained coveralls and put him to bed in his clerical collar, shirt and pants. "Somehow it doesn't seem right to undress his Reverence while he's asleep," Tom said, so they just covered him with a blanket, turned off the light and left.

CHAPTER FIVE

Man Is Born to Trouble (One More Time)

CARLO ENTINI'S prelude, Sunday morning, proved to be a mournful dirge instead of his usual galloping Bach. The choir processed to the joyous hymn, "For the beauty of the earth, for the glory of the skies. For the love which from our birth, over and around us lies. Lord of all to Thee we raise, this our hymn of grateful praise."

By the time they had reached the third measure, Andrew knew he'd chosen the wrong hymn. When he looked out at the congregation and saw the large crowd of young people, he was afraid he'd chosen the wrong topic. Feeling for the customary glass of water at the pulpit, he was sorely tempted to take one of his unaccustomed tranquilizers, but remembering how the first one had affected him three days ago, decided against it. It did nothing for his confidence to see several young people with notebooks. Tom Packney was seated next to a bouncy blonde who could only be Her Nibs the Bibs. She was adjusting her tape recorder. Andrew wondered if the New York *Times* were represented.

The young seminarian finished reading the morning Psalm which was 104, the psalm which blesses the Lord as the creator of the earth, making it fruitful, sustaining it. Words Andrew had never heard in that psalm before leaped out at him.

"The trees of the Lord are watered abundantly, the cedars of Lebanon which he planted.

In them the birds build their nests; the stork has her home in the fir trees . . .

O Lord, how manifold are thy works! In wisdom hast thou made them all;

the earth is full of thy creatures . . .

When thou hidest thy face, they are dismayed; when thou takest away their breath, they die and return to their dust . . ."

Nothing like a psalm about the birds and storks and creation to set the stage for a sermon about abortion, thought Andrew, rising to read from Ecclesiastes.

"For everything there is a season, and a time for every matter under heaven. A time to be born and a time to die: a time to plant and a time to pluck up what is planted . . ."

He gained confidence as he read, and shortly he smiled at his assembled flock and plunged headlong into "A Season for All Men." His delivery was magnificent. His timing was poor beyond belief. The first person at the door to greet him was a stringy-haired young girl about seventeen.

"Oh, Dr. Mahoney, you've given me the courage I need to ask my parents for an abortion. I know they'll say yes now that they've heard you. This sermon will change my entire life!" She wrung his hand and moved on.

"Dr. Mahoney, let me wish you a very good morning and a

very goodbye." It was Gerald Watkins speaking. "I shall tender my resignation to the session first thing tomorrow morning. You, sir, have struck a blow for permissiveness that even the liberals across town never dreamed of. My family will never enter this church again."

Andrew began to count them. Six against and one for . . . five against and one for . . . six against . . . then there were none. He stood alone at the door of the sanctuary, the cold wind whipping at his long black cape. And then he saw them. Seven shiny mice on seven stair steps leading to the balcony. It was the family of Jeremiah Malachi Mouse. For a moment he had the feeling they were going to attack him, then he closed his eyes. When he opened them, the mice were gone.

Monday is traditionally a minister's day off, so Andrew didn't go near Bellview Presbyterian Church even to collect his mail. Rather, he spent the day tidying up his living quarters, rearranging the furniture which the Women's Association had arranged, and buying food at the local A & P. Had he but known it. he'd have been better advised to go to his office, for it was in the aisles at the A & P that he heard the reviews of his Sunday sermon.

While reaching for a can of tuna fish he heard two women angrily denouncing the minister's stupidity in preaching such a sermon when many college kids were home on midwinter break. At the cream cheese counter he heard two teen-age girls giggling about the sermon. He averted his head as much as possible and ended up with only eight items in his basket, enough to qualify for the express check-out line. He was in no mood for an instant replay of his abortion sermon.

He realized he'd stirred up a hornet's nest but nevertheless he felt himself justified in having delivered it. He could only speak what he believed. Hadn't he always stressed to his students in Interpersonal Relationships that they must be "true to themselves?" Don't sell out to pressure groups, he had told them. Base your beliefs on Biblical content and everything else will fall in line. Don't just preach what the people want to hear, otherwise how would you ever educate the congregation? All these things he mulled over as he sipped a cup of instant coffee and put away his eight items. He knew he'd have to visit another grocery store. Maybe he'd try the little Stop 'n Go later this evening.

It was 3 p.m. when the doorbell rang. Standing at Andrew's front door, shivering in the January cold, stood Tom Packney, friend of friends.

"Oh, come in, Tom. What brings you out this way?"

"You only live a block from high school, or hadn't you noticed? I stopped by to give you this advance copy of the *Bell Tower*. It'll be distributed in school and in town Wednesday, and I thought you might want to look it over before some of the parents get their hands on it. You're kinda famous, you know, Padre? Wait till you see what Bibs wrote about you. They've even got your picture. Oh, didn't you see the photographer taking your picture there at the end of the sermon? No, I guess you didn't, 'cause you were giving the benediction."

Andrew sank into his only overstuffed chair. Tom had barely paused for breath in his non-stop recital, and now he shoved a four-page edition of the school paper at his new friend. Of the four pages, one entire page was devoted to the Reverend Dr. Andrew Pinkham Mahoney, his sermon, "A Season for All Men" and letters to the editor about it. Heading the feature article, by-lined Elizabeth Hanlon, was a three by four picture of himself, head erect, eyes closed and right hand raised in benediction. Tom backed out the door, waving as he went. Andrew picked up his lukewarm cup of coffee. He read:

New Prophet Appears on the Local Scene
    "At the Bellview Presbyterian Church on Sunday we were treated to something different in clerical dissertations. The Reverend Dr. Mahoney, himself new to this area, preached on the subject of abortion. He really had nothing new to offer on this provocative and timely subject, but the fact that it was presented from a pulpit gave one the idea that it had the endorsement of Christ or Moses or, at the very least, the General Assembly of the Presbyterian Church. And Rev. Mahoney speaks with an authoritative voice but does he carry a big stick? He may shortly be in need of one when the conservative parents rally round.

    "Briefly, he sanctioned a woman's right to have an abortion, based on the Supreme Court decision of January 22, 1973. Based further on the passage from Ecclesiastes that says there is a time for all things; a time to be born and a time to die; a time to plant and a time to pluck up what is planted, etc.

    "Now there is a new concept for the sex ed courses: once a father plants the seed, does a mother have the right to pluck up what is planted? How fortunate that Abraham and his wife didn't feel that way when the Lord said to him, 'You shall be the father of a multitude of nations.' She was goodness knows how old. The mother of Christ could have made a good case for abortion. After all, she wasn't yet married. And that, Reverend Dr. Mahoney, is where your wicket is sticky. You've given carte blanche to any young girl who might have been considering abortion; or one who might have been considering having a seed planted. Remember, you heard it first at Bellview Pres."

There were other articles by lesser staff members and several letters to the editor. Most of the authors indicated vociferous support of Andrew's position. Instead of feeling better, Andrew began to feel angry. He felt even angrier when Tuesday's issue of the *Bellview Times* came off the press. Out of seven letters to the editor, six were against Andrew's stand on abortion. One was bemoaning the school budget. There was no covering news article on the subject. Presumably none of the *Times* staff were members of his church. He considered writing a letter of rebuttal but changed his mind. He decided to let the chips fall where they may.

At his Wednesday evening meeting of the church session chips fell when almost any subject was brought up for discussion. Gerald Watkins had sent in his resignation. They couldn't decide on a replacement. Since Andrew knew only a handful of people in the church he was of no help but relied upon the advice of Jim Logan and Bill Gordon. The women were all in favor of adding another female to the group of elders. It was a real hassle, nothing was decided and Andrew developed a splitting headache. He forgot to ask for or offer a closing prayer.

Apparently they were all accustomed to this procedure anyway, so they stood quietly when Andrew rose and Bill Gordon prayed.

"Our Heavenly Father, we praise your name, your Almighty name, and we thank you for choosing to call us your children. We thank you for every single circumstance surrounding our meeting here tonight; the difficulties, the dissension, the division. Because we know you are working out your plan in our lives, and we praise you for closing one door in our faces, knowing you are ready to open another and better one. We lift up your Son Jesus and thank you for His saving grace. We wait upon you, O Lord, and ask that you dismiss us in your love and care. Amen."

From the lounge closet, Jeremiah, Timothy, Peter and Reginald bowed their heads and murmured "Amen." Reginald immediately coughed to show that he hadn't meant to say it. He didn't really know why he'd allowed Jeremiah to drag him to this silly meeting. He'd never before in his life heard so many people speak so many words on so many subjects without arriving at satisfactory conclusions.

"People should be seen and not heard," he told Timothy.

They remained in the closet until all members departed. Timothy asked to be excused to practice the organ. Reginald said yes he'd remain for a cup of whatever it was Jeremiah was going to offer him.

"Carrot tea, is it? No brandy? Well, I think I'd better shove off. I've got the night shift at the Bakery. You know, ever since we joined the union I've been getting stuck with the night shifts. But the foreman says they need big fellows like me to keep down the cockroaches, and it does pay well. How else could I afford my bachelor pad at the Hardware Store?"

Said Jeremiah, "I'm fortunate to be getting morning shifts at the Bakery and Delicatessen. In order to feed and clothe my brood I have to hold down two Jobs." He pronounced Jobs with a long o and was immediately interrupted by Peter the scholar. "Not Jobs, Pater, jobs. They're two different words. Job is the Biblical word, and job is — "

Jeremiah continued unabashed, "That, coupled with keeping things in order here at the church sometimes gets me down. But I don't accept pay for my work at the church, you know. Our family have always been church mice and quite poor in comparison to other mice. But we have our pride, and we do fend for ourselves. Wouldn't have it any other way."

When Jeremiah finished speaking, Reginald was half out the door. What a long-winded fellow that Jeremiah was. It all comes from living in ecclesiastical quarters for a lifetime. Sermons were notoriously lengthy, Reginald knew. That's mainly why he'd stopped going to church. And then, nobody was very friendly. He stepped over a mousetrap just aft of the basement door after carefully extracting the cheese.

"You've got the eyes of a cat," his mother always told him. "But see to it that the cat doesn't get yours!" Yes, Reginald could evade most any trap that man might devise. All of Jeremiah's family had so far been successful in not being trapped. His kids were well-trained, one had to admit.

Jeremiah and Peter sat alone in the lounge nibbling at some cooky crumbs the session members had spilled. Jeremiah poured himself a small cup of tea, added milk and sugar and sat on the rim of the cup to drink it.

"Call your mother up, Peter my son, and say to her that something detaineth her lord and master. I don't feel called to return to the fold as yet. Yea and verily, something troubleth my insides."

Peter pushed down the intercom button and dialed the number for the kitchen. His mother answered immediately. "Hello, Mother," said Peter. "Peter, where have you and your father been? The session meeting should have been over long ago."

"The session meeting is over, but Pater and I are having a cup of tea. Then I think we will stop by the library for a little bit."

"Don't stay up too late. Your father has to be at work at six in the morning."

"All right, Mother. Goodnight."

Peter looked up to find his father watching him. From his perch on the tea cup Jeremiah said to his son, "That prayer Mr. Gordon said tonight sounded a lot like the one you prayed last week in the broom closet. Do you think perhaps he's been reading the same books you have?"

"Indeed, yes, Pater. It was he who gave the books to the library."

CHAPTER SIX

A Gathering of Two

PETER AND JEREMIAH washed their tea cups and turned off the light in the lounge. Using Peter's flashlight, they made their way down the darkened hall toward the library. Twice Jeremiah slipped and slid on Tom Packney's freshly-waxed floor.

"Drat that Packney! Why must he over-do everything? He over-waxes, over-vacuums, over-"

"Never mind, Pater. The library is carpeted and won't give you any trouble. Here, let's light a candle so as not to attract passers-by. This may take some time."

"What, my eldest son, may take some time? I proposeth merely to glance through these new books you mentioned. I'm tired and sleepy. These session meetings weareth me to a nub."

Peter took four books from the bottom shelf and put them on the carpet. Finding the page he wanted in one of them, he sat on the opposite page to hold it in place.

"Now Pater, uh — actually I think I'm going to start calling you 'Father.' If that's all right with you. It seems more suitable somehow."

"Quite suitable, I'm sure, seeing that I'm your father. I never really cared for that 'Pater' jazz, if you must know."

"Now, Father, you're familiar with the New Testament and the Acts of the Apostles?"

"Like the back of my paw, son. But only from the King James Version. I wouldn't give you two cents for some of the versions that read like last night's newspaper."

"They do reach some of the younger generation who don't dig 'thees and thous and verilys', because they have the virtue of speaking in the vernacular to the masses."

"Are we speaking about the same church, son? I don't recall masses being said in the Presbyterian Church."

"Father, don't be obtuse. I mean the congregation at large. Now back to the Acts."

They each opened their Bibles; Peter, the Living Bible, and Jeremiah, the King James.

"Let's each read the first two chapters in Acts, Father. Silently, of course."

They read silently, except Jeremiah frequently opened and closed his mouth, nodding occasionally in agreement. It always relaxed and soothed him to read the Holy Scriptures. It was his manna from heaven. It was this very manna that had nourished his family and his father's family before him. There it was they found strength to oversee the inner workings of the churches where they lived and to earn their daily bread. Finally Peter broke the silence.

"Do you believe what you've just read in those two chapters, Father?"

"Believe? Of course I believe, son. How can you ask your old gray-haired father a question like that?"

"It says when the 'believers met together that day,

suddenly there was a sound like the roaring of a mighty
windstorm in the skies above them and it filled the house
where they were meeting. Then, what looked like flames or
tongues of fire appeared and settled on their heads. And
everyone present was filled with the Holy Spirit and began
speaking in languages they didn't know, for the Holy Spirit
gave them this ability.' You believe that?"

"Yea and verily! I believe that was the beginning of the
early Christian church. I believe miracles followed after, and
then Peter, that son-of-a-Jonah, preached a sermon to the
Israelites that day that would take the fur off a cat!"

"Great! So do I! Do you believe those things still happen
today: people receiving the Holy Spirit, speaking in unknown
languages and performing miracles through the power of
God?"

"No."

"Why not, Father?"

"Because we don't see it happening, do we? We don't hear
about it, do we? That's why I don't believe it happens."

"Do you think it *could* happen today?"

"Oh, it could happen, all right, if God wanted it to. He
can do anything, you know. But I doubt if he means churches
like this to have it. What would they do with it? They've got
a thousand Christians on the rolls already."

"But you surely agree, Father, that sitting in a pew doesn't
make a man a Christian. Not a born-again Christian.
Anyway, you know yourself that only a handful of those
thousand come on Sunday."

Jeremiah began to get a touch of indigestion from the tea
he'd drunk. He felt his stomach gurgling and his toes
tingling.

"What are you trying to tell me, son?"

"I'm trying to tell you, Father that what we've just read
does still happen, because it happened to me last week."

"*What* happened?"

"I've been reading these books that tell exactly how people, including a few here in BPC, have received the baptism in the Holy Spirit and who speak in 'other tongues.' After I'd read the books and looked up the references in the Bibles, yours and mine, I decided to ask to receive the Holy Spirit."

Jeremiah's stomach was now on fire. He felt like a volcano about to erupt. "But son, you're a mouse. Didn't you know that? And the Bible was speaking about people. Apostles. Disciples. People."

"We are God's creation, Father, just as surely as Adam and Abraham. Genesis 1:24: 'And God said, Let the earth bring forth the living creature after his kind, cattle, and creeping thing, and beast of the earth after his kind: and it was so.' I Timothy 4:4: 'For every creature of God is good, and nothing to be refused, if it be received with thanksgiving.' Mark 16:15: 'And he said unto them, Go ye into all the world and preach the gospel to every creature.' Try looking up Colossians 1:15,16 and also verse 23. Those are all from your Bible, Father. Look up Hebrews 4:13 and Romans 8:19–21."

"But Peter, my son — "

"If God had meant just people he'd have said just people, but he said 'creatures'! We're living creatures, Father, from his Almighty hand. Praise the Lord!"

"And the baptism — "

"I prayed just as this book suggested. I asked God to forgive me of all my sins; asked Him to remove from my life all things not acceptable to Him; asked Him to empty me out and fill me with His Holy Spirit and to pour out His blessings in abundance upon me."

"And He did?"

"He did!"

"How do you know?"

"Because I felt His Spirit come upon me, and I began to praise Him in a language I never knew. You know that I've learned Greek, Latin, French and Spanish. It was none of those. Oh, Father, it was so beautiful! I did so want to share it with someone else. Oh, I'm glad you decided to come in here tonight. I couldn't have contained myself much longer." Peter was speaking with so much excitement that his glasses began to jiggle on his nose, and his breath made the candle flicker.

Jeremiah was swallowing rapidly, afraid he was going to ask the question he knew he would ask. But first he had to know what other signs Peter had been given.

"Father, I prayed that God would put a wall of protection around us all so that we might escape the traps, and you know not one of us has been caught, though we've successfully taken the cheese. And I also asked the Lord what He wanted us to do as a result of this baptism."

"Us?" Jeremiah felt faint.

"Yes. He revealed to me quite clearly that you will be the one to show Pastor Mahoney the way to the spiritual baptism."

"Me?"

"Yes, Father. Do you wish to receive the Baptism in the Holy Spirit now so that God can begin working in you?"

"Son, I wouldn't mind having the baptism. I'm not one to stick at receiving a gift from God. But I don't want to speak in any other language. I'd feel foolish. What will Reginald say?"

"He'll say 'Praise the Lord!' after you tell him about the baptism and after you ask God to heal his sciatic leg. You wouldn't want to deny him the joy of waiting for the glorious coming of the Lord, would you? Romans 8:22 in the Living Bible clearly says: 'For we know that even the things of nature, like animals and plants, suffer in sickness and death as they await this great event.' "

The battery in Peter's miniature flashlight burned out and only the flickering candle lit the library. It cast faint shadows on the floor and on the rows of books. Peter still sat on the opened book, three other books stacked beside him. His father sat on the floor facing him, looking quite queer in the face. His whiskers twitched slightly. Then Jeremiah bowed his head, kneeling as only a mouse can kneel and said to his son, "I'm ready when you are."

Peter laid his paw on his father's head and asked him to seek the Lord's forgiveness for any unrepented sins. Jeremiah did so. Peter began to pray.

"Heavenly Father, holy be your name. Worthy are you to be praised. Alleluia! We sing praises to you forever. Now, Heavenly Father, in the name of your Son Jesus, if there be any spirit here that is not of thee, we pray that you will cast it out. Before you kneels my earthly father, seeking to be baptised in your Holy Spirit. Most merciful God, pour out upon him your blessed Spirit, just as you did upon the disciples at Pentecost, through your Son Jesus Christ. Fill him with your love and grace; grant him gifts according to your desires and let him begin to serve you and to praise you in the language of your Spirit. Thank you, God. Thank you, Jesus. Thank you, Holy Spirit. I believe that you are doing this now. In Jesus' name. Amen."

Jeremiah's indigestion suddenly ceased. He felt peaceful and warm all over. He opened his mouth to ask Peter if that was all there was to it and found himself using words he'd never in his life heard before. He found himself praising God softly, quietly, then loudly.

He didn't know what he was praying, but God knew. He didn't know if he'd ever be able to stop, because he wanted to laugh and dance and sing and play the harp and the cymbals. Now he could understand King David and his mighty urge to praise God in all ways. He wanted to praise him forever! But abruptly he was made aware of his mouse knees so he said, "Thank you, Lord," in English and rose up.

"Here am I, Lord, send me," he said quietly.

Peter put the books back on the shelf and blew out the candle. Fortunately, the books had been on the lower shelf and were easy to return to place. His father grabbed him by the paw.

"Your mother will have a fit because we're so late. We'd better start praying she doesn't wake up."

"She won't waken, Father. I've already prayed."

They went down the hall together, two quite different mice than they were two hours before. Peter walked sedately, bubbling inside. Jeremiah skated over the slippery floor, bubbling all over. Peter smiled to hear his father praising God for Tom Packney's wax job.

CHAPTER SEVEN

Give 'em the Acts!

EARLY the next morning, Jeremiah slipped out the door of the church kitchen and headed for his job in the Bellview Bakery. He would work until noon in the bake shop while the fresh breads and cakes were being made, then from noon until three p.m. in the deli, nosing out ants and insects and fumigating the place. As he made his way past the Hardware Store he met Reginald coming home from his night shift. Jeremiah honestly didn't know whether or not he could face rugged Reggie this early in the morning, after the experience he'd had the night before. Should he tell Reggie or not?

Reginald, puffing on a miniature pipe, began as usual to complain about everything. It was damp at night in the Bakery. He was allergic to the cinnamon they used in the coffee cakes. He hated roaches and bugs, and how were things in the Mousetrap Presbyterian Church?

Jeremiah cleared his throat. "Um, uh, quite well, Reggie.

Exceedingly well, in fact." He wasn't aware that he wore a rather mystifying smile, but Reggie was and this puzzled him.

"Can't think what you've got to look so happy about. If you had my sciatica and this cough, you wouldn't be smiling, I'll be bound." Here he coughed to show that he really had one. "But then, you always were an odd one. Why do you stick it out over there? You could move into the beauty salon any day, I happen to know, and avoid the persecution."

"The Lord God is providing protection for us. Not one hair or whisker of my family has been harmed."

"Well, he very nearly let *me* have it as I left your place the other night. Just missed getting into a trap by that much!"

"Why don't you come over tonight, and we'll talk about it?"

"What's Priscilla having for supper?"

"Tuna souffle."

"I'll be there in time for supper, then. A bachelor's lot is not an easy one, eating alone all the time. Good day to you, Jeremiah." Reginald tipped his green plaid cap in Jeremiah's direction and sucked on his pipe. Given another bill in back, he'd look like a ratty, bumbling Sherlock Holmes, thought Jeremiah. A chronic griper, a thorn in the flesh, one who'd try the patience of a saint; Reggie was all this and more. Then Jeremiah dismissed the thought as unworthy of a mouse who'd prayed in the Spirit. He asked his Maker's forgiveness. He had, in fact, a very hard time settling down to work. He seemed to want to sing all morning.

Miriam Maxom was also having a hard time settling down to work. She typed and retyped copies of the minutes of the session meeting. It was so frustrating to find little holes in the carbon. They looked like tiny teeth marks. Patti Barnum was home with a cold and Dr. Mahoney hadn't yet arrived. There'd been such a to-do over his abortion sermon, Miriam wondered what topic he'd chosen to preach on the next Sunday. She was a little worried that people were not finding him acceptable, and that was too bad. He was really very nice.

She flushed a little; oh well, what if she were a few years older — three, four? If only he didn't get discouraged and leave, or worse yet be removed, before she had time to prove herself attractive and trustworthy. She pictured the pale lavender writing paper she would order from Macy's with bold purple initials on it: M M M. Or should it be m M m? In any case, it would be lavender.

"Good morning, Miss Maxom." It was himself standing in the doorway.

Miriam flushed even brighter, "Good morning, Dr. Mahoney. Your mail is on your desk, and the coffee pot is perking." Abruptly, she knocked a sheaf of papers off the desk, and Andrew stepped forward to pick them up.

"Did I get any calls this morning?"

Miriam consulted a small pad at her elbow. "Only one. A lawyer named Frederick Harlowe called, representing Mr. Gerald Watkins. Mr. Watkins is suing the church to recover the special gift of three thousand dollars he donated to repair the furnace. He claims he gave it in good faith to what he believed to be a conservative church, and under no circumstances would he help finance a liberal one."

Andrew merely smiled. "Thank you, Miss Maximum."

Miriam did a double-take but he'd blithely gone out the door, unaware that he'd mispronounced her name. She was furious. Just wait until I get my hands on that Tom Packney, she raged. He overdoes everything, even his sense of humor. The idea of telling the minister he called her Miss Maximum!

Luckily for Tom, he had band practice that afternoon and didn't receive the punishment she'd prepared to dole out. Miram was so furious, so frustrated, she called the hair salon and made an appointment to have her hair frosted after work. It had been six months since her last frost job. I'll show them! Miss Maximum, indeed.

Without Tom Packney's help, elderly Mr. Walters was having slow going cleaning the Sunday School rooms. He was further hampered by having to stop in strategic places and re-bait the mousetraps.

"For the life of me I can't figure out how the cheese is taken, and none of the traps ever sprung."

What with the price of cheese going up daily he felt compelled to call to Dr. Mahoney's attention that this was a waste of time and money. Dr. Mahoney didn't take the advice too kindly. True, for the moment he'd stopped hearing the voices, but mice occupying the premises was not to be tolerated.

"But Reverend," objected Mr. Walters, "churches have always had mice since time began."

"Talking ones?"

"Well, now, I don't recall ever hearing one talk. But then I don't hear any too well." Mr. Walters shook his head as the minister walked away. This new man was hard to figure. "Old Mr. Hanagan never heard voices, and he was almost my age," murmured the old caretaker as he swished away with a wet mop at the kitchen floor.

Inside the kitchen cabinet which was home to the Mouse family, this conversation was overheard by Priscilla, John Mark, Phoebe and Baby Mary who were lunching on that classic church delicacy, the covered-dish casserole. Mice commonly consume almost anything edible, and Jeremiah's family was no exception: seeds, vegetation, meat. Today they enjoyed a tasty concoction of sunflower seeds au gratin, John Mark's favorite. At the moment, he was hanging by his tail from a cup hook near the door, the better to hear the voices outside.

John Mark turned to Phoebe and said, "Guess it's about time we hit him with another dose of high decibel squeaks. Won't do for the minister to get complacent. If he doesn't hear us, and he can't catch us, he's missing all the fun."

Phoebe agreed. Priscilla cautioned them both. "Children, I'd advise you to be careful. Very careful. Peter seems to have staked out all the traps but suppose he overlooked some? Anyway, why do you want to heckle the poor man? Hasn't he got enough trouble after his sermon on you-know-what?"

Flippant Phoebe replied. "That sermon on abortion was a real flopperoo. I've read lots more interesting data in the New York *Times*. I'll lay you ten to one he preaches on euthanasia next week."

Priscilla was so shocked at Phoebe's language she dropped a tea cup. "Phoebe, how could you be so crude? Your grandmother would turn over in her grave if she could hear the language that issues from your mouth! And besides, Baby Mary heard you say a-b-o-r-t-i-o-n."

"Mother," John Mark laughed. "You don't need to spell around Baby Mary. She can't even read or write yet. You're being over-cautious."

Phoebe said in an aside to John Mark, "Did you notice how Timothy has changed his position on abortion since the Reverend M. preached? At first he was gung ho in favor, now he's swung around the other way. He's like a weathervane, that Timothy. I think he musta got his tail caught in the organ pedals." She and John Mark laughed, and Priscilla felt obliged to shush them.

"Mums, is it okay if I go over to visit Saran after dinner? She's gonna do my nails and frost my hair after the beauty shop closes."

"All right, Phoebe, if you can conduct yourself like a lady. But you must all be present for dinner. I'm making tuna souffle. We're having a guest for dinner Papa said."

"Who? Sir Reginald the Rat?" John Mark asked.

"He's a d-r-i-p if you ask me," said Phoebe as she flounced off without helping with the luncheon dishes. This left John Mark to help his mother and to take Baby Mary for her airing in the little mouse carriage, a thing he hated doing. Privately he vowed to leave home very soon if this sort of thing kept up. Just because he wasn't the student Peter was, nor the musician Timothy was, nor the gadabout sister Phoebe was, it was totally unfair that he, John Mark, ended up so many times as nursemaid. But he loved his mother, and so reluctantly wheeled Baby Mary out the kitchen door and lifted her carriage over the doorstep and out onto the sidewalk. Surely Mother would miss him when he left, but he doubted if the rest of the family would.

"They're all selfish, selfish, selfish!" He liked the sound of the words so much that he made up a little rhyme that he could say to the rhythm of the carriage wheels.

> "Sel-fish is as sel-fish does,
> I shall leave my home becuz,
> Sel-fish brothers, sel-fish sister,
> My left paw has got a blister."

He went round the block one more time changing the words slightly.

"Sel-fish man with sel-fish trap,
Sits with Bible on his lap,
He may be to his dismay,
Caught in his own trap some day."

Then abruptly he swung into, "London Bridge is falling down, my fair lady!" John Mark had completed two turns around the block, had walked off his hostilities and had arrived at the kitchen door. Also, the germ of a plan had taken root in his mind. He decided to postpone running away for the time being.

As soon as Miriam Maxom finished work she made a beeline to the hair salon across the street. Hot on her heels went Phoebe also heading for a frosting. Sara Ann, sister of Elma Evelyn Kathleen McMouse, knew the technique quite well by now and had established a small but elite clientele. It bothered her not at all that the salon furnished the frosting and the nail polish. The jobs she took after the shop closed provided Miss McMouse with pocket money, but she had a very small pocket and charged very little for her services.

This evening her only appointment was with Phoebe. She liked Phoebe well enough, although it irritated her beyond words when Phoebe called her "Saran" instead of Sara Ann which was the proper spelling of her name. Phoebe insisted she'd seen the name many times in the A & P, and it was always spelled "Saran."

"Someday I shall frost her in emerald green instead of the pale lavender she likes so much. That would certainly fix her wagon!" Phoebe slipped in through a small hole in the ventilator and joined her friend in the storage closet which is where Sara Ann worked. Only a thin wall separated them from the main salon room which Miriam had just entered.

Two other customers were in the front of the salon being cut, set and dried. Working girls like Miriam took their appointments in the evening. Philip, her hairdresser, greeted her with a big smile.

"Miss Maxom, how nice to see you! We've missed you lately."

"Oh, I've been tied down with extra typing and dictation," Miriam said. "I can't seem to get away for two hours in the daytime like I used to do."

"I understand things have changed somewhat at your church. Do you like the new man? What's his name?"

"Mahoney. The Reverend Dr. Andrew Pinkham Mahoney."

"Wow, that's some title!" Phil remarked as he put the plastic cap on Miriam's head. He took a needle-like hook and began to lift out strand after strand of hair through small holes in the cap. Miriam squirmed. This was the part she liked least of all. She would gladly have dropped the subject of Dr. Mahoney, but Phil was bound to continue.

"Your new pastor is even making waves at St. Barnabas, where I go. Couple of the younger priests have taken their cue from him and are speaking out on some moral issues that have been taboo traditionally in our church. The older parishioners don't like it, you understand. What do your people think?"

"He's only been there a few weeks, so it's difficult to tell. But we have had three couples leave the church and one who's threatening to sue to get his pledge back."

Phil laughed and in so doing yanked at a strand of hair harder than he meant to. "Ouch!" Miriam said, as tears gathered in her eyes.

"Sorry about that. It just struck me funny that someone would sue to get his money back from a church. I never heard of that before. Do you think he'll get it?"

Miriam wiped her eyes and remarked that it didn't look

too likely, as part of it had already been spent on furnace repair.

"If they don't finish repairing it, we'll really be out in the cold," was her attempt at humor.

"If your church were really on fire, you wouldn't need a furnace!" observed Phil as he worked a creamy lather into the strands of hair.

"What's that supposed to mean?"

"You know, on fire — like the New Testament churches. On fire with the Holy Spirit. Then they'd have so much power they could turn off the heat and the electricity and never miss 'em!"

"I guess that must be some sort of joke, but I don't get it, and I'm quite sure Dr. Mahoney wouldn't."

Phil reached into a drawer under the counter and handed her a small book. "Have you heard of the charismatic renewal that some churches are experiencing today? It's happening in Catholic and Protestant churches alike."

Miriam shook her head, and Phil said, "Take a look at this little book while I do a shampoo. It will give you an idea of what I'm talking about." He left her to bleach while he shampooed another client. Miriam poured herself a cup of coffee from the large urn on a shelf and leafed through the book. She recognized some of the verses from scripture, yes — some of her very favorites were there, but it was all tied in with a lot of unfamiliar expressions and ideas and she had trouble concentrating on it. She read again the RSV translation of I John 3:1. "See what love the Father has given us, that we should be called children of God; and so we are." But what did it mean to be a child of God? Are we all children of God, she wondered? She put the book aside and picked up the evening paper.

Miriam didn't see Phoebe and Sara Ann peek at her

through the louvres of the swinging doors. Sometimes they perched on the doors to get a free ride as the beauticians went in and out from the supply room. Also it helped speed up the drying process.

Phoebe was saying to Sara Ann, "She's sweet on the new Reverend at our church. But he can't see her for sour apples. I'd say she's gonna be an old maid."

"She's not bad looking," remarked Sara Ann, who always liked to give credit where credit was due.

"Looks aren't everything, you know, Saran. She's icicle-stiff, super-efficient and given to clumsiness, if you get the picture."

"I don't exactly. How can you be super-efficient and clumsy at the same time?"

"She's efficient with machines and typing and filing, but around men she comes unglued."

"Maybe she ought to get Phil to pray for her."

"Pray for her?" Phoebe almost lost her balance on the swinging doors.

"Oh, he'll get around to it. He prays for a lot of the customers. Sometimes they tell their hairdresser things they wouldn't tell their best friends. Some of these gals have got real problems. It's kinda eerie how a lot of them work out when he prays for certain things. Hey, here he comes. We better get you rinsed off before he sees us." They made a quick exit, as Phil entered the room to pick up a bottle of hair conditioner.

The evening wore on. Phoebe's frosting was completed before Miriam Maxom's, but the little mouse decided to stay and sip a cup of Sara Ann's carrot tea. Anyway, her nails were not quite dry. What she was actually hoping for was to hear the hairdresser pray for Miss Maxom. Wonder how he'd go about it? She broached this subject to her friend.

"About this praying for Miss Maxom — d'ya really think Mr. Phil might do that?"

"He would if she'd ask him."

"Maybe she doesn't know she's got a problem. If you call being a clumsy old maid a problem."

"He's pretty keen, Mr. Phil is. He senses a lot about people. Sometimes I don't know what he's praying about though."

"Well, Saran, if you hear him why don't you know what he's saying?"

"Because, Pheeb, he doesn't always pray in English."

"He prays in Italian?"

"I don't think it's Italian. Sometimes I hear him and another hairdresser, Miss Madelyn, praying together and they call it 'praying in the Spirit.'"

"Sounds ghostly to me. Well, I think my nails are dry, Saran, and I'd better get going. I forgot Momma wanted me home for tuna soufflé. Eek! I'll bet she's mad. How much do I owe you?"

Sara Ann figured out the bill: frosting (ears and tail extra) shampoo, set and manicure. "That comes to a dollar and a quarter. I won't charge for the tea."

"Thanks a lump, Saran. You've gone and raised your prices. Last time it was only a dollar."

"You know everything has gone up in price, Pheeb. Supplies are hard to get."

"Oh, sure, you have to go all the way to the third shelf to get your bleach, don't you? Does Arturo know you use his equipment?"

"He would if he ever asked. Since he doesn't ask, I don't say. That way, everybody's happy. Goodnight, Pheeb."

"I wish you'd call me 'Phoebe.' I much prefer it to 'Pheeb.'"

"I feel the same way about 'Saran.' "

"Oh, all right. Goodnight, Sara Ann. Here's your tip."

Phoebe slipped out just ahead of Miss Maxom. She couldn't tell if the secretary had been prayed for or not, but she really had a neat frosting job. She carried two books Mr. Phil had given her, suggesting she might like to leave one on Dr. Mahoney's desk. Miriam had no intention of leaving anything on Dr. Mahoney's desk except the morning mail. Would Katharine Gibbs offer advice to Norman Vincent Peale?

Phil was clearing away the towels and trays in the salon, when he heard a little rustle behind him.

"Come on out, Sara Ann. I know you had a frosting tonight. I could hear you girls."

This was the first time he had ever acknowledged Sara Ann's presence, and it startled the little mouse so that she dropped the tip Phoebe had given her. In dismay she watched it roll under the hairdresser's foot. He picked it up and put it into Sara Ann's pink pocket. Then he also picked up Sara Ann and set her on the counter. He took a chair in front of her.

"Now, Miss McMouse, it's time we had a talk. What do you think we ought to do about the amount you're charging your customers?"

"Do?" It was a barely audible squeak that the wee beautician managed.

"Yes. How much do you think you should reimburse Arturo for the use of his supplies and equipment?"

"I — uh — ah — "

"I guess twenty-five percent ought to cover the expenses. That will still leave a nice profit for you, Sara Ann, and you really do an excellent job, you know. Would you like to work on people?"

Sara Ann gave him a startled look. Was he serious? Then she saw he was smiling, so she smiled too.

"Say, you're pretty nice, Mr. Phil. I guess I am relieved to be an honest mouse again. I always had a nagging feeling that it wasn't quite right. But I didn't know you could see me. Does anyone else know I'm around?"

"Only Madelyn, and she won't tell. Now scoot along home will you, and I'll see you tomorrow morning at nine o'clock. On the dot, remember!"

Sara Ann ran home to join her family at the Pharmacy. She had a very warm, tender feeling around her little mouse heart. Soon, she thought, I'm going to ask him about those books he gives to people and ask him how to pray. "Maybe I'll start on Miss Maxom myself. Hm-m-m, maybe I will."

CHAPTER EIGHT

Mirabilia!

WHEN MIRIAM, freshly frosted, returned to the church parking lot for her car, she saw a light still on in the minister's study. Though she wanted to stop by her office and pick up the package of spaghetti dinner she had bought at noon and left in a desk drawer, she couldn't risk meeting Andrew Mahoney while carrying "that book." He would notice. He would ask. And what could she say? My hairdresser sent you some suggestions for sermons? Not likely!

Instantly revising her dinner menu, she unlocked her blue Chevelle and headed for her apartment a mile away. She felt absolutely drained of energy. That was one reason she rarely had her hair frosted, but moreover, she had the feeling of being spied on all the time she was in the salon.

Parking her car in back of the building, Miriam took the self-service elevator to her second floor apartment. She always got a great deal of pleasure when she entered her own private sanctuary. The furniture, Mediterranean, was her own. The color scheme and decor were also her own. Antique gold carpet, bronze satin draperies and pumpkin walls accented a bronze velvet couch.

Tonight she slipped out of her shoes and headed for the sparkling mustard and cream-colored kitchen. She made herself a cup of Chinese tea and two pieces of whole-wheat toast, took them into the living room and turned on the television. The "super-efficient" secretary removed her purse and gloves from a big gold chair, tossed them on the floor and flung herself into it.

She was tired of being efficient (or clumsy) depending upon whom she encountered, tired even of being secretarial. She sipped her tea, sans milk, and nibbled at her buttered toast. Because she had neglected to turn up the sound on the TV set all she got was a colorful talk show with no talk. It wasn't worth the effort to stumble over and adjust the volume dial.

She picked up one of the books Phil had given her. Its blue cover had a brilliant sunburst of golden lights splashing over it. *Nine O'Clock in the Morning*[1] by Dennis Bennett — odd title, she thought. Miriam glanced at her watch. "Hm-m, just nine o'clock at night. What have I got to lose?" She opened the book and sipped at her tea.

Three hours later, Miriam Maxom, sitting on her feet in the gold chair came to the realization that a flag was waving on Channel 2. Presumably someone was singing, "The Star-Spangled Banner." She switched off the set and started into the bedroom.

After one fleeting glance at the white and gold bed, she returned to the living room and opened a storage closet disguised as a frescoed wall panel. She began to dig into various boxes on the shelf and on the floor. By now her stockinged feet were getting cold and she felt hunger pangs in her middle. She dug further, tossing out blankets, Christmas tree decorations and out-of-season clothing. "Miss Super-efficient" let everything lie on the floor until she came to what she was after, her mother's family Bible.

"I'll clear it away tomorrow," she announced to no one in particular. "Or maybe I won't!"

She returned to the table by the gold chair and picked up the blue book. It was then that her compulsion to neatness took over. She returned to the closet, repacked all the boxes, stacking them on the shelves and floor. All were neatly labeled according to the contents. Why then, she wondered, didn't one bear a label reading, "Mother's Family Bible in Here?" Maybe that was because she had scarcely looked at it since her mother gave it to her six years ago.

In the bedroom, Miriam carefully pulled down the blue satin cover, folded it and laid it to rest on the blue satin bench at the foot of her bed. Then she undressed, removed her makeup, brushed her teeth, slipped into a blue flannel nightgown, covered her hair in a pink net cap and got into bed.

No good; she was wide awake. She opened the Bible to the New Testament. Starting in Matthew, she read through the twenty-eight chapters in the King James Version. She thumbed through to the Acts of the Apostles and read the first four chapters. Then she skipped about: Romans 8; I Corinthians 12, 13, 14 and back again to Acts 2. Her heart was beating so loudly in the quiet room she could hear it above the ivory and lavender china clock on her bedside table.

"He was right. That man was right. It's all here." Then she began to wonder if Phil knew all this was in the Bible. "All this" being Jesus' crucifixion, resurrection and ascension. Did Phil know about the power that came upon the apostles on the Day of Pentecost, when the tongues of fire touched their heads and they began to praise God in heavenly languages? What was it Phil had said?

"If your church were really on fire, you wouldn't need a furnace!" On fire with the Holy Spirit. Then we could turn off the heat and electricity and never miss 'em. That's what he'd said.

He *knew!* Praise God, he knew!

Miriam got out of bed, took off her fluffy nylon cap, slipped her feet into fuzzy blue slippers and knelt beside the French Provincial bed. She began to cry softly. Then she cried as though she'd never stop. She sobbed and watched the tears rain down on the pale blue electric blanket, wondering vaguely if they might short it out and start a fire.

A fire! "O God, that's what I want. A fire! I want to be on fire for you. To believe in you so much I'll never be lonely or tired or worried again.

"God, I'm so tired! So tired of typing and filing and never feeling happy or loved or that I'm doing something for you. What good is my typing those dumb old reports and letters? Lord, show me a better way to serve you.

"Heavenly Father, you know my own father has been dead for six years. I still miss him, but I remember what it was like to have a loving father. Dear Father, let me come to you tonight and ask your forgiveness for my sins; my selfish sins, all the things that keep me from putting you first in my life. I believe in your Son Jesus, and I believe that you will do this for His sake.

"Empty me out, Lord, and refill me according to your purpose. Whatever you tell me to do, I'll do it. I really will. Let your Holy Spirit come into my being and start a fire in my life. O thank you, God! Thank you, Jesus! Thank you, Holy Spirit!"

Miriam still knelt beside her bed. She couldn't hear her

heart pound now. She didn't hear the clock. She didn't even see the clock, for her eyes were caught on a bright splash of light hovering in a sparkling circle on the blue curtains. It glowed like a thousand candles, flickered briefly and faded as quickly as it had come.

Miriam started to thank the Lord but she only said three words in English, followed by a soft waterfall of mellifluous sounds — the tongue of angels, perhaps.

So it was that Miriam Maxom, child of God, crept into her blue bedlinens at two-thirty in the morning, wearing her fluffy blue slippers and without her fluffy pink cap. She smiled, fell instantly into a deep sleep and didn't awaken until six-and-a-half hours later. It was exactly nine o'clock on Friday morning.

Phil, hairdresser extraordinary, walked into Arturo's Salon at exactly nine that morning and remembered events of the night before. Before starting his first shampoo of the day, he slipped into the storage closet and whispered, "Thank you, Lord, for giving me a chance to witness to Miss Maxom last night. Thank you for letting me pray for her. Praise you for preparing her heart to receive your Holy Spirit."

Sara Ann, mouse extraordinary, was already at work in her part of the storage closet. She smiled to herself as she heard the prayer. "I must ask him to do that for me tonight. Now I won't need to start on Miss Maxom. Maybe I'll start on Phoebe!"

Jeremiah Malachi Mouse left the bakery at nine a.m. for his coffee break. Since he didn't drink coffee, he perched on a sunny rock in back of the Pharmacy and took the air. Alone here, gazing into a deep blue winter sky, he felt how good it was to relax and just be a mouse — an ordinary, gray furry mouse. First he curled up on a flat rock and let his tail hang off. Then he strolled along a piece of dead wood, letting his long tail drag behind. Next he leaned back against an old tin can and scratched his stomach. Ah-h! A pleasure so great it was almost sinful! That brought him to the remembrance of dinner last night, when Reginald Rat had given them his interpretation of original sin. "My Lord, what a night!"

In spite of Reggie's rankling words, Jeremiah felt he wanted to praise the Lord. He began to speak to God in his new prayer language, squeaking mightily to heaven of his joy and thanksgiving.

"Who said that?" a voice practically in his ear inquired.

Jeremiah turned and saw no one. He continued to pray and sing in the Spirit. The voice came again.

"I say, is that you, mouse, doing that singing?"

Then Jeremiah saw a rusty-capped field sparrow chirping at him from the fringe of weeds in the lot back of the stores. Gazing at the mouse with rather a blank expression, the pink-billed bird got off a series of sweet, slurring notes that ascended into a sharp trill.

"Did you address me, bird?"

"Indeed, I did. Couldn't help it. Most unusual to hear a mouse singing in the Spirit. I assume you've had the baptism."

Jeremiah was flabbergasted!

"Do birds know about singing in the Spirit?"

"Of course! Who do you think made the very first music when the world was created? Birds!" The sparrow lifted up its head, puffed out its chest and quoted from Genesis. "The Spirit of God moved upon the face of the waters . . . and there was light and darkness."

"And God called the light Day and the darkness he called Night," responded Jeremiah.

The bird answered with the next verse, and so they continued through the first chapter of the first book of the Bible.

The sparrow eyed the mouse admiringly. "You certainly know your Bible, mouse."

"Call me Jeremiah, friend. And what's your name?"

"My Latin name is *Spizella pusilla pusilla*, but you may call me 'Enrico.' Praise the Lord!"

Jeremiah knew then why God had his eye on the sparrows all this time. No wonder! The very first singers in the Spirit. What joy! Wait until Reggie meets this young fellow, thought the churchmouse. Lousy sparrows indeed! He'd change his tune, no doubt.

Jeremiah thought that he himself might take wings and fly, as he caught a vision of what it might be like when the "Spirit shall be poured out upon all flesh." When that wondrous joy had spread to all the people in the churches and in the town; when they all stood ready, the people, the mice in the church, the cat in the grocery, the birds in the branches, the dog in the gas station and even the flowers in the park — all ready and waiting for Jesus to come.

"Oh, I shall mount up with wings as an eagle!" sang Jeremiah in a remarkably fine tenor voice.

"If you don't get frostbitten first," called out Enrico, as he circled low over Jeremiah's head and then flew off in the winter sunshine, leaving a fluttery vapor trail in his wake.

CHAPTER NINE

A New Broom

PHOEBE, eldest daughter of Jeremiah Malachi Mouse, lost her bet concerning the next Sunday sermon. The Reverend Dr. Andrew Pinkham Mahoney didn't speak on euthanasia. His sermon topic was based on his attempts to upgrade, update and generally revive Bellview Presbyterian Church. He thought it best to acquaint the entire congregation (at least those who came on Sunday) with his plans.

He proposed to rid the church of its "dead wood" by pruning the rolls of inactive members. Further, he had decided to eliminate heretofore essential services such as calling on every member of the congregation. Emphatically, he stated that his own calls upon members would be limited to those of an emergency nature: sickness, death, urgent counseling. If the budget could not be met, they would operate on the monies received as long as possible; when the money ran out, the services would run out.

"The first program we will have to eliminate will be church

school for children of inactive or non-member parents. We may have to institute a tuition fee for children of member parents. We may have to hire teachers, making more of a drain on the budget, if the volunteer staff gets any smaller."

He advised the music director to choose only anthems and special music from those they already had. No new music, no new choir robes.

"We will pay essential salaries and for heat and light in the building. All else will be considered luxuries."

His closing prayer was one of desperation. "Lord, help this church to survive if you have further plans for its people. If there is a remnant here which you would draw out, we ask you to do so, in the name of your Son Jesus. Amen."

The mouse family, seated on a railing in the balcony, nudged each other.

"Ask and ye shall receive," said Jeremiah.

"Seek and ye shall find," said Priscilla.

"You have not because you ask not," said Peter.

"I'm hungry!" said Phoebe.

Chatting together for a few minutes after the service, Jim and Sue Logan and Bill and Carol Gordon also nudged each other.

"If he keeps on asking, he's going to get it!" said vivacious Sue, eyes twinkling.

"But does he know what he's asking for?" her husband wondered.

"By the way," Bill Gordon said, "I wonder if any of our books have ever been checked out of the library. Let's nip downstairs and take a look. I'm interested in knowing if anyone's read them."

In the deserted library the four scanned the bookshelves.

"Hah!" Carol was the first to spy them. "They certainly didn't put them at eye level, did they? Here they are on the very bottom shelf."

Her husband took out the books and checked the cards in back. "Well, I don't see any names on the cards, but these certainly look like they have smudges and prints. Someone's been reading them, that's for sure."

"Look at this," said Sue. "Here's a piece of Swiss cheese someone used as a bookmark! How about that?"

"At any rate," Carol remarked, "somebody's looking at them, even if they're not checking them out. And that's good. I wonder who it is?"

As they started to leave Bill made a suggestion.

"I think it's time we got our group together and started really praying about this. You know our friend Mahoney is riding for a header unless the Lord reins him in."

"I agree," said Sue.

"I'll call everybody," said Carol. "Where shall we meet and when?"

"How about Tuesday night in the Upper Room?" It was Sue's suggestion, and they all agreed.

The Upper Room of the Bellview Presbyterian Church was a small unused former office/former library/former church school room directly above the furnace. It was reached by a short flight of steps from the hallway that led to the kitchen and to an outside entrance. The door was kept locked to discourage vandals, but Jim Logan had a key.

At the moment it was partly a storage room, with church school supplies sitting in one corner and a closet full of seasonal decorations and equipment. It had the disadvantage of being too warm, winter or summer, located as it was over the heating system, so no church groups were inclined to use it. Many of them had forgotten it even existed, since this part of the church belonged to the original building which was erected in 1929. The sanctuary and offices, choir rooms and meeting rooms had been added several years later.

Here it was that eleven people met on a cold Tuesday

night in February, 1975. Not all those gathered were members of the church but belonged rather to the fellowship of Charismatic Christians within the community. The Gordons and Logans were there. Three members of a Presbyterian church in a neighboring town, two Catholic friends and two teen-agers from BPC comprised the group of eleven.

A faded blue rug covered the floor, and most of the people sat on that or on cushions. There were four chairs and a couple of yellow stools someone had borrowed from the church kindergarten room and never returned. The overhead fixture didn't work, but a floor lamp standing in a corner provided enough light. Some bare white bookshelves lined one part of the back wall. An ambitious unknown decorator had painted the other walls a garish shade of blue.

As nominal leader of the prayer group, Jim Logan took charge. "Better leave the door ajar, Bill. It's so darn hot in here, we'll need a bit of air. Just open it a little, that's okay. Nobody'll be around here tonight anyway."

Everyone settled down. The two men and one woman from Fairfield Presbyterian Church introduced themselves to the members they didn't know. "I'm Fred; this is Ralph and his wife, Jane."

The Gordons and Logans knew everyone. Donna McCarthy and her friend Art Carroll, the high school seniors, were introduced to the two women from the Catholic church.

"Donna and Art, this is Mary Herman and Mary Ann Coburn. Now that we all know everybody I'll tell you why I called the group together. To be perfectly frank, there's only the six of us in this church, so far as we know, who've experienced the renewal in the Holy Spirit. We need prayerful support for this church and our pastor. We've pitched in to help each other on several occasions when there's been a special need or a special prayer request. So we felt you'd all be willing to uphold us in this."

Everyone smiled and nodded. "Praise the Lord!" echoed around the room from several people.

"Is there anyone who'd like to share some special thing the Lord has done in your life since we last met?"

A general time of sharing and fellowship began that gladdened the hearts of all.

"I have some scripture, I'd like to share with you," Jim said. "Today I was praying that God would lead us in the meeting tonight and asking Him if there was any hope of spreading the word about His Holy Spirit here in our own church, in our own town and this is what He showed me. Hebrews 10:23–25:

" 'Let us hold fast the confession of our hope without wavering, for he who promised is faithful; and let us consider how to stir up one another to love and good works, not neglecting to meet together, as is the habit of some, but encouraging one another, and all the more as you see the Day drawing near.' "

"Praise the Lord!"

"Bless his holy name!"

Bill Gordon began to pray. "Our Heavenly Father, how we love you and adore you who speak to us through your Holy Word. Praise your wonderful name! Praise and thank you, O God, for bringing these friends, your children, here together to share in fellowship to receive the blessings you have in store for us. Hear our requests as we pray for this church and for other needs of your family of men. In Jesus' name, Amen."

"Dear loving Lord," prayed Sue Logan. "We hold up before you this church and its pastor, seemingly bound and determined to alienate himself from us all. At the same time, O God, he sees the need here in the empty lives and empty pews. O God, empty him out and fill him up with your Holy Spirit. Take him in hand and make him see that the only way back is through the very door of heaven. Remove his pride of intellect, his impatience, his ill feelings, and show him, Lord, what a church on fire can be. Spare none of us, Lord, down to the smallest creature, but bring us all anew to your throne of mercy and use us in whatever way you will. In the name of Jesus. Amen."

Sometime during the middle of Sue's prayer, three small mice crept into the room unnoticed. Peter, Timothy and frosted Phoebe. They had seen the light and heard the murmurs.

"Spare none of us, Lord, down to the smallest creature," the words were barely out of Mrs. Logan's mouth when Phoebe, following her two brothers, stepped into one of the Reverend Mahoney's traps just in back of the door. The *snap* of the trap sounded in the quiet room like a thunderclap. Phoebe's shrill squeak of pain and fright was magnified a hundred times. Peter and Timothy looked up to find Jim Logan standing above them.

"What have we here? I didn't know the church had mice and mousetraps."

He stooped down to rescue Phoebe and set her on her feet. The little lavender-frosted mouse couldn't stand, however, and began to moan in pain. Timothy was so frightened he could only gulp. Peter knelt down beside his sister and began to stroke her leg gently. He bowed his head and closed his eyes. Then he prayed in his soft, sweet, spirit language, partly singing, partly moaning. He could see that her right front paw was dangling oddly, broken probably.

Jim Logan saw it too, and when he'd recovered from his surprise at hearing a mouse singing in the Spirit he joined in. The other members of the group moved closer, and a beautiful hymn of spiritual praise rose above them. For several minutes they praised God in a spiritual song; one note blending into another, all unknown to everyone. Just as abruptly as it began, the song ended; quite as though an unseen conductor had wielded a baton signifying the finish. Peter was thrilled beyond words.

Now Peter was praying to God in his ordinary language.

"Dear Heavenly Father, one of your small creatures has fallen in pain and anguish. Lord, we know that you're more ready to give than we are to ask; you know we want Phoebe's paw and leg to become straight and well. We ask this in Jesus' name and for His sake only. Thank you, God."

Jim Logan was also stroking the frosted mouse who still lay motionless, moaning softly.

With a sudden surge of faith, Jim said, "In the name of Jesus, I declare that your leg and paw are healed and ask you to rise up in His name! Amen!"

Phoebe's leg began to twitch slightly, then rather rapidly. She rolled over from her back and righted herself, prepared to run. Were these not enemies? Something made her wait. Something about Peter and the big man who knelt beside him.

"I suppose we should be surprised to find church mice who pray in tongues and pray for healing. But somehow I can't be too surprised. How long have you had this spiritual blessing, young man?"

"For only a few weeks," said Peter. "My father has received it, too."

"So has the hairdresser at Arturo's!" Phoebe chimed in.

Everyone laughed. Timothy was red with embarrassment.

Peter introduced himself, Timothy and Phoebe to the group.

"The Reverend Dr. Mahoney set the traps for us, because it upset him so to hear our voices. We've been very successful in evading the traps. This is the first accident we've had, and I do thank you and your friends for praying for my sister. See,

she's as good as new." Phoebe, the center of attention, took this opportunity to execute a few dance steps.

"Would your sister and brother like to receive the baptism?" Jim Logan was still spokesman for the group.

Peter consulted his family. Yes, they thought they would like that. Someone placed the two young mice in the middle of the blue rug. Peter stood between them, with a paw on each head. Jim and Sue Logan explained to Timothy and Phoebe what they must say and do.

Phoebe was so excited, she thought her little heart would pound right out of her frosted body. Now, she thought, I can pray for Miss Maxom so she needn't be an old maid. And for Saran, uh, Sara Ann, also. "Praise the Lord!" she whispered under her breath.

Timothy tried hard to be very dignified but succeeded only in looking like a mouse who's about to burst for joy. He prayed softly to himself while Mr. Gordon prayed aloud that he and Phoebe might receive God's Holy Spirit. For want of sophistication and people-type hangups, the two young mice began immediately to praise God in an unknown language. Mr. Logan knelt down to hear Phoebe pray, and she placed a damp kiss on his cheek.

Then she, Peter and Timothy ran out, squeaking together in a Spirit-filled song. They raced down the short flight of stairs and ran headlong into Reginald Rat.

"Well, if it's not the Three Blind Mice!" said that worthy. "Watch out where you're going!"

Poor Reginald lost his balance during the collision and had trouble regaining it. The three mice sailed on unaware. Then Peter returned and took Reginald's paw to steady him.

"Here, Uncle Reginald, let me assist you."

"Uncle Reginald, is it? What have you three been up to? I've a mind to tell your Pa."

"Oh, we are going to tell him, Uncle Reggie. As soon as we deliver you to the kitchen and make you comfy."

"Young man, I haven't been comfy in years! Who could be comfy with this sciatica? Hey, watch it, there's a trap."

They were all glad to assemble at last in Priscilla's warm kitchen. Baby Mary was asleep in a plastic butter tub, covered with a pink paper napkin. Her small bottle dangled carelessly from a milky mouth. Around the table, which was tonight an empty rice box, sat John Mark, his mother and father. At the arrival of Peter, Timothy and Phoebe, accompanied by their erstwhile neighbor, Jeremiah stood up and made room for four more occupants. He dragged up a matchbox for Timothy and Peter, two boxes of toothpicks for Reginald and Phoebe.

"Mother," Jeremiah said to his wife, "brew a little more tea, will you?"

"And put a shot of brandy in mine," said Reggie. "The night air has made my leg worse, and I had the misfortune to collide with three unidentified flying objects. My cough is always worse in the evening dews and damps." He was all set to tick off his troubles for another several minutes when Jeremiah interrupted.

"We've got no brandy, Reg, but here's a shot of molasses that should do as well." He dribbled a few drops of molasses into Reggie's cup and after a few sips, Reggie decided it wasn't half bad. Probably had more vitamins, anyway.

"Now let us convocate here together to begin evening vespers and a time of sharing and fellowship," the mouse father began to leaf through his Bible for an appropriate scripture. Phoebe was having a stricture.

"Papa, Papa, there's something we've just gotta tell you guys. Wait till you hear what happened upstairs!"

"Sis, I don't know if this is the time — " Peter began.

"It is too the time, and I'll tell Papa all about it!" Timothy had jumped in.

"No, it's my story and my leg, and I'm gonna tell it!" Phoebe was adamant.

Either Jeremiah had found his scripture, or he was quoting from memory. "Lo, children are an heritage of the Lord; and the fruit of the womb is his reward. As arrows are in the hand of a mighty man; so are children of the youth.

"Happy is the man that hath his quiver full of them: they shall not be ashamed, but they shall speak with the enemies in the gate. Psalms 127:3–5."

"Jeremiah!" It was Priscilla's voice, as stern perhaps as she'd ever addressed her lord and master.

"Jeremiah, for once I wish you'd forego the thees and thous and speak in the King's English! I can't make head or tail of it, and I want to hear the children's story."

Shocked though he was, Jeremiah felt he had to protest. "My dear, this *is* the King's English. Good King James."

"Then let the King take a back seat. I want to hear what happened to my daughter's leg. Out with it!" The whole family was shocked to hear this impatient tone coming from the ex-cathedral mouse mother.

Peter spoke. "It's as Father said, Mother. We were speaking with the enemies in the gate. Only they weren't really enemies but brothers in Christ."

"Jeez," Reginald was about to give up. "You sure know how to keep a guy dangling. What in blazes is this all about? The enemies in the gate? What gate?"

"A figure of speech, sir. You see, Mother and Dad, we three slipped upstairs to the small room over the furnace, when we heard some voices up there tonight. You know it's been a long time since anyone used that room, and we were curious. No sooner had we gotten into the room and hid behind the door, when Phoebe stepped into one of the minister's traps."

"Oh, my Lord!" It was Mother Priscilla. "Were you hurt?"

"Oh, yes, Mother, hurt badly!" Phoebe assured her.

"What actually happened, Mother," Timothy felt obliged to continue the story, "was this: when Phoebe stepped into the trap, her paw and leg were twisted, and she was in great pain. One of the men lifted her out and it was clearly apparent that her limbs were broken or badly mangled."

Priscilla began to cry.

"It's all right, Mother." Peter took charge again. "The people upstairs prayed for her healing, and her leg straightened out and became whole again."

"The people upstairs?" Jeremiah was baffled. "Do you mean — ?" He looked heavenward.

"I mean the men and women gathered in that little room upstairs who are this minute praying and singing in the Spirit. It's a bunch of Charismatic Christians!"

Reginald's ear detected a familiar sound. "Did you say sciatic Christians?"

"Reginald, you know perfectly well what my son said." Jeremiah was determined not to have a duplication of last night's dead-end conversation. "We must bow our heads and give thanks to our Maker for the safe return of our prodigal daughter. Though she were trapped, yet she is free. Though she were in pain and agony, now she rejoiceth. Though her limbs be crooked, He hath made them straight. Blessed be the name of the Lord! All praise and honor and glory to Him who can heal a little mouse. The same who yesterday tended the smallest sparrow, today careth for a mini-mouse. Praise ye the Lord!"

One by one the mouse family said, "Amen!" Then one by one they excused themselves. Timothy felt he must play some Bach to settle his nerves, and truth to tell, he felt like composing a cantata of the miracles he had seen this very night. Peter meant to search the scriptures and other books in the library for more on the gift of healing. John Mark was recalling the plan he'd formulated a few days previous. Would this be a good night to carry it out?

Priscilla washed the tea things and smoothed out Phoebe's bed. The little dear should get her rest this night, after that most unusual experience. Priscilla was almost beginning to understand what Jeremiah and Peter were talking about.

"I don't really need to understand it, though. I just need to believe it. That's enough for me." The mouse mother spread the bed with a lavender napkin — Phoebe's favorite color. She heard Reginald depart in high dudgeon — again. That made the second or third night in a row. Jeremiah ought to shake the dust of his feet off Reggie and not bother any longer, she felt. He (Reginald, that is) was a stubborn, hard-hearted, closeminded old bachelor. He didn't deserve the patience and kindness Jeremiah gave him.

"If he were married, he'd be very different, I'm sure," was her earnest conclusion. But she remembered Reginald's oft-told motto, "I'd rather be dead than wed." She just shook her head sadly.

CHAPTER TEN

A Message from Arturo's

FOR A week following her baptism in the Holy Spirit, Miriam Maxom had moved "the book" from one desk drawer to another, had actually laid it on Dr. Mahoney's desk once and then had run back to retrieve it. Now wasn't the time, she kept telling herself. He'd be certain to question her about it, and what would she say? She hardly knew herself what had happened; how could she hope to explain it to a theologian from Wedgewood Divinity School? She made another appointment at Arturo's.

Phil could tell by the look on her face that something had happened to the mousey Miss Maxom. Her face had a real shine to it. She looked like a little girl who'd had a birthday and Christmas at the same time.

"You read it!" he said, as he lathered her frosted locks. With her head hanging backward over the shampoo sink,

Miriam nodded and smiled. "Did something happen?" he asked her. Again she nodded and smiled.

"I have a million questions to ask you," Miriam began the moment she was seated in front of the long gilt mirror. "Tell me what happened to me."

"It's simple," said Phil. "You just laid claim to a promise in the Scripture which says that Jesus will baptize in the Holy Spirit. He released what was within you already, when you became a Christian and were baptized in the name of the Father, the Son and the Holy Spirit. Now you are ready to be used by God fully. The "more abundant life" mentioned in John 10:10 is on the way! Tell me what's happened since."

"I've had this unbelievable peace ever since. As though nothing could touch me. I'm really reading the Bible for the first time, seriously. It all sounds so different now . . . so true!"

"Amen! You have to read it daily, study it, get yourself involved in a Charismatic prayer fellowship. We have one at St. Ignatius every Friday night at eight," Phil paused. "Did you leave the book with your minister?"

"No, I haven't yet. I'm sort of scared to."

"Well, I'll pray for you to have the courage. You'll get bolder, as you get older in the faith. You know what I mean? When you're a "born-again", spirit-filled Christian it's like you're new . . . an infant again. And you have to grow on the Word, become nourished with grace and faith. Soon you'll be seven feet tall!"

"Gracious," laughed Miss Maxom. "I hope not! But I think I understand what you mean. You know, you sound more like a preacher than our — uhm, than, most preachers! Have you got any more of those spirit-filled books?"

Phil answered by opening a drawer next to her and removing two small books. "Take these, they'll help explain all about what's happened to you and where to find all the scriptures you need to back up your faith. Now, I'll put you under the dryer next to Emily Ardmore. See what you can do for her. She's got a sick husband and an unmarried pregnant daughter. And come to think of it, she goes to your church!"

Usually, Miriam found it difficult to hear anything or to sustain a conversation while under the dryer. But today when she smiled at Emily Ardmore, Emily smiled back and asked, "Aren't you Miss Maxom from the church office?" Miriam said yes, and asked how Mr. Ardmore was getting along. She remembered from the church sick list that he was recovering from a heart attack.

"The doctors say he isn't out of the woods yet, Miss Maxom. He looks so bad. Every time I go to see him in the hospital it just breaks my heart."

Big tears suddenly welled up in Emily Ardmore's eyes and fell on the book in her lap. Miriam glanced down and saw with surprise that it was one of Phil's "spirit-filled" books. She wondered if Emily had experienced this renewal. Somehow, they both managed to dry while talking back and forth under the noisy dryers that looked like big pink cages over their heads.

Miriam discovered two things about Emily: she was only a few years older than Miriam, and her car was disabled so she had no transportation to the hospital that day. No mention was made of her pregnant daughter, but Miriam gathered that the family life was in a turmoil over the husband's health, finances and general desperation. Miriam decided to act. Her first impulse was to offer her car to Emily for the day, but right on the heels of that thought came a more forceful one, "Take her!"

Reason took over and she felt herself thinking, "I can't leave the office in the middle of the day. It was stretching a point to come over on my lunch hour. I can't possibly be finished before one-thirty. But I can lend her my car."

The still, small voice became more insistent.

"Take her!"

"Mrs. Ardmore, let me take you to the hospital this afternoon to see your husband. We can grab a sandwich next door at the deli after we're combed out and go on from there."

"Oh, Miss Maxom, that would be wonderful. I was going to ride the bus, but it just takes so much longer that way. How can I ever thank you?"

Emily's dryer went off, and Phil started the comb-out. Miriam took another ten minutes to dry, got a quick comb-out, and she and Emily left Arturo's arm-in-arm, headed for the deli next door. Miriam's still, small voice was silent but she had a knot in her stomach. How was she to tell Dr. Mahoney that she wanted time off to take Emily to the hospital? This was the afternoon she was to prepare his session notes.

"The Lord will provide," she murmured to herself in her new-found faith. And that's exactly what He did.

While Emily and Miriam were lunching on grilled cheese sandwiches, Tom Packney and Bibs Hanlon were screeching into the church parking lot in his Volks. Tom leaped out of the car at once in order to open the door for Her Nibs. He caught her with one leg half out the door; clearly, Miss Hanlon hadn't kept company with a true gentleman lately. She smiled her appreciation and allowed him to carry her notebooks into Dr. Mahoney's office. That gentleman had (reluctantly) granted her an inerview, which she hoped to make biographical. Having flayed him with her typewriter during the abortion dilemma, she felt she owed him the courtesy of a more comprehensive article.

What made the man tick? Was he ticking or smoldering? These and other questions had plagued her of late. She looked forward with great glee to the hour he'd granted her.

Tom offered to escort her, which she considered kind of him. Also she gathered that Tom had become especially fond of the Padre.

Andrew Mahoney had finished his lunch; a bologna sandwich he'd put together at home, lathered with mustard and relish, and had just concluded a very unsatisfactory telephone conversation with Miriam Maxom. Calling as she was from the deli, he could hardly hear her over the din of coffee cups and conversation. It appeared she wanted the afternoon off to take somebody to the hospital to visit a sick husband.

"And what shall I do with my session notes, Miss Maxom? This is also Patti's afternoon off, and I've no one to type them."

"The Lord will provide, Dr. Mahoney. Besides, I'll be back by four at the latest."

"Very well, Miss Maxom, but I do hope this isn't going to become a habit."

Miriam thanked him and hung up, leaving him to wonder just how the Lord would provide? Such naïveté was quite unsuited to a secretary.

"Come in," he called, in answer to a triple knock at his study door. Miss Elizabeth Hanlon entered, followed by Tom Packney. A genuine shiver of apprehension flowed through the minister's spine. He felt momentarily as though he'd admitted his own executioner.

The effervescent Miss Hanlon, clad in blue jeans and a white wool jacket, thanked him for the hour he'd allotted her. She assured him she had her questions all lined up and was prepared to waste none of his valuable time, and could they please start immediately?

"As a matter of fact, Miss Hanlon, it looks like we'll have to be very brief or postpone this meeting altogether. Miss Maxom, my secretary, just phoned to say she won't be in this afternoon, and my session notes aren't transcribed for tonight's meeting. I just don't see how I can spare the time right now, as it appears I'll have to type them up myself."

"Well, then — let me first type off your notes while you and Tom have a cup of cocoa from this thermos we brought along, and in ten minutes or less we'll be ready to start the interview. Okay?"

Without waiting for an affirmation, Bibs picked up the sheaf of yellow papers lying on the minister's desk. In bold printed letters the title read SESSION NOTES, all else was virtually illegible. Bibs could barely suppress an audible "yick" when she saw his miserable handwriting. She asked Tom to show her where the typewriter and supplies were. Dr. Mahoney watched her blonde curls bounce up and down as she trailed tall Tom Packney back down the hall to Miriam's office.

"Gee, Bibs, this is great of you to type the Padre's stuff. Bet this'll soften him up for later on. Are you sure you want to do this?"

"Tom, I never wanted to do anything more in my whole life. In fact, I'd spend the next year of my life with the Australian bushmen, if I could only *read* this mess. Oye! Such handwriting."

"Don't worry, Bibs. You'll do it. I'll pray for you while I'm pouring the Padre's cocoa."

"Pray for me? Well, pray do!"

Tom had wiped out the tea cups from the silver service on the table in Andrew Mahoney's office and was pouring the cocoa when Bibs buzzed in to ask the minister how many copies he wanted.

"Actually, Miss Hanlon, what I need is a stencil and twenty-four copies run off on the mimeo. You probably can't handle all that right now, can you? So why don't we forget the whole thing, and we'll set a time for the interview next week?"

"Dr. Mahoney, if you'll still give me the interview when I'm finished here, I guarantee you'll have your stencil and mimeos very shortly. I'm holding a space in the *Bell Tower* for this article and we go to the printer tonight. Is it a bargain?"

"Right on, Miss Hanlon. Right on!" There was a laugh in Andrew's voice over the intercom, and Bibs wasn't sure but what he was saying, "Write on! Write on!" What difference? First, she had to read the blasted stuff. "What I wouldn't give for a translator!"

Phoebe, in her customary spot in the filing cabinet, heard the entire conversation and pieced in what she wasn't sure about. One thing was certain, Miss Hanlon needed help deciphering Dr. Mahoney's handwriting, and Phoebe meant to come to her rescue. If there was one thing she was an expert at it was reading his writing. Even though he'd only been at BPC for a few weeks, Phoebe had come to know every scrawl, swirl and squiggle of his notes. She hopped out of the cabinet and perched herself in back of the pencil holder on Miss Maxom's desk. She had a clear view of the minister's notes and a clear channel to Bibs Hanlon's ear. In her sweet little mouse whisper she began to read them off so clearly and distinctly that Bibs thought she herself was doing it.

"Wow! This is easier than I thought. What luck!"

She sailed through the stencil, three pages, as it turned out. Not wishing to disturb Tom and the "Padre" she decided to start the mimeo on her own. "Thank God I took that business course this term."

"Yes, that's what you should be doing, thanking God!"

Bibs shook her head. "Don't tell me I'm hearing voices." She adjusted the paper, and she heard it again.

"You couldn't have done this, you know, without God's help. You should praise Him and thank Him for everything that's happened. You are an instrument of His peace today."

The unshakable Miss Hanlon felt very queer and shook-up. Where was that little voice coming from? She looked around for a cassette or tape recorder she might have turned on by mistake.

"Thank Him, Miss Hanlon!"

"Okay, already! Thank you, God, for letting me get into this mess on account of I'm so smart and had to have that follow-up article on his Holiness. Thank you for the fact that he's probably bored to tears with Tom and may walk out on the whole deal in a few minutes. But thank you anyway that I'm cracking up and won't be able to get the school paper out on time."

By the time she'd said all that, Bibs was crying, didn't know whether she was mad or sad and saw quite unexpectedly a lavender-striped mouselet expertly feeding the paper into the mimeo. She saw, too, that twenty-four copies had been made and the machine was being turned off. She looked at her watch. Twenty minutes had elapsed since she had left the minister's office. Bibs laid the papers neatly on the table and started to faint.

She never reached the floor. A little mouse voice was saying, "Hold her up, Lord. I know you've still got work for her to do. Hold her up! Praise the Lord!"

Bibs raised her head off the table as she'd only sunk part way down, grabbed the papers and ran down the hall. "What a creepy place!"

In the minister's office she said, "You've got mice in here, Dr. Mahoney. Did you know that?"

"Yes, Miss Hanlon, I know that. But their days are numbered." He paused to count the copies she had made. "I don't know how you managed in such a short time, but

I really admire your tenacity. In the face of such an accomplishment, I can only say "thank you," and hope that I can give you something worthwhile to write about."

Tom excused himself to wash the cocoa cups, while Bibs whipped out her tape recorder and notebook. Thirty-seven minutes later she was finished. It had taken exactly one hour, portal to portal, to enter Andrew's office, do the copies, get the interview and sashay out.

"I really do thank you, God," Bibs said silently as she loped along behind Tom Puckney. Tom squeezed her hand, as he helped her into the car. "You know, I think the Padre was eating out of your hand when we left. I believe you two will be great friends."

"I wouldn't count on it," Bibs replied, as they wheeled out of the parking lot and into the busy street. "But thanks for your help. Actually, I had a lot of help today." She was remembering the lavender-striped mouse. I must have been hallucinating, she decided. A lavender-striped mouse she could believe (barely) — but a talking mouse? No way!

Miriam Maxom and her new friend, Emily Ardmore, were waiting in the small, secluded lounge on the fifth floor of the cardiac unit in the intensive care section of Marlinberg Hospital. At ten minutes of the hour, Emily went in to see her husband. When the ten minutes were up she waited again until the next visitation period. She and Miriam talked quietly. Mostly, they talked about Phil, the hairdresser.

Emily said, "He's really been a big help to me. More so than anyone else. We have no family here and no really close friends. Dr. Mahoney stopped in once to see me, but he didn't have much to say. Remember his abortion sermon?"

Miriam could hardly forget.

"Our daughter, Monica, heard that sermon, and she took it to be complete assurance that she should get an abortion. She's pregnant, you know. Seventeen, and pregnant. Not married, just pregnant. . . ."

Her voice trailed off hopelessly. She seemed to be saying what did it matter, what did anything matter?

"On top of everything else, money's getting to be a problem with Frank not able to work. Anyway, thank God for Blue Cross."

"Thank him for another kind of Cross, Emily!"

They exchanged glances. "Now you sound like Phil. He's always telling me to thank God anyway. I just can't do it! I'm bitter, and I know it. How can I thank God for all that's happened to Frank and Monica? Oh yes, I've read the books Phil gives me, but I just can't thank God for this."

Miriam, newly-born into the kingdom of God, a mere infant in the faith, slipped into the background, and the Holy Spirit spoke through her. Never in a million years could she have found the words to help this woman in need.

"But it's praise and thanksgiving that open the door to God's great mercy, Emily. I've been reading so much about that in the Bible lately. You know, in the Psalms, King David was always praising God even when his enemies were all about him. I found in the Old Testament, I think it was Second Chronicles, that certain priests were appointed just to be singers and trumpeters to praise and thank the Lord in Solomon's temple.

"No, I don't think God makes the bad things happen to us, but I think He uses them to strengthen our faith and to accomplish His purpose."

Emily was clasping and unclasping her hands. "Sometimes I feel like Job. There's someone I can really identify with."

Miriam exclaimed, "Oh, I wish I'd brought my Bible. I

haven't yet gotten brave enough to carry it to the beauty parlor! Only last night I was reading Job, and you know, his story ended in triumph. At the very last it said that God turned the captivity of Job, when he prayed for his friends. When Job's attitude changed from bitterness to repentance, God restored his blessings."

A man sitting opposite them was listening intently to their low-keyed conversation. He's Jewish, thought Miriam. Well, it won't hurt him to eavesdrop a little. She raised her voice a smidgin.

"I don't pretend to understand all of these things, but as far as I've come in the Spirit, and that's not far, mind you, it seems to boil down to this: the Bible is true; it means what it says. When the prophets said way back in Isaiah and in the Psalms that the Messiah would come, He really did come. And because we were sinful and couldn't inherit the kingdom of God, that Messiah, the one they called Christ, became the scapegoat for us; died for us. Like Phil says, if we believe that and accept that sacrifice and the fact that God raised Him from the dead, then we can become children of God. Then we are ready for God to work in us. To do through us the things he did through his first disciples — miracles, healings, teachings . . ."

Miriam began to tremble inwardly. A warm, all-encompassing glow spread throughout her whole body. She felt as though she were being bathed inwardly in a golden sunbath. It suffused her arms, legs and passed out through her hands and feet. Emily looked at her to see why she had stopped speaking. The Jewish gentleman raised his head from the newspaper he was reading. The waiting alcove was deathly still — silent.

Miriam felt that her face must be mirroring what was happening to her, and she wondered if she, too, might be having a heart attack. Perhaps I'm dying, but I don't care, because I wouldn't trade this moment for anything in the world. Three times the golden, suffusing glow filled her being and flowed out through her fingers and feet. She grabbed Emily's hand. She prayed aloud.

"Oh, Heavenly Father, whatever it is that you are doing to and through me, I thank you and praise you for it. Oh, show me what to do next, for I feel that your Spirit is here now, but I don't know what to do."

Very softly, Emily began to weep, then she also prayed. "Dear God, I praise you and thank you, too. Thank you for Frank's condition. I know now you didn't cause him to be ill, but I truly believe you are using this to bring us both closer to you. Right now I'm willing to let you do with me what you will, and if it means giving up Frank, I'll trust you in that, too. I love you, Lord! Thank you!"

The two women embraced and sank to their knees. In a new, sure voice Miriam began to speak to God.

"O God, our Father and our Maker, thank you for Jesus, our Healer and our Savior. Right now we are asking you to heal Frank of his infirmities. Make his heart strong and lively once more. Restore him to his home and family, so that your Son may be glorified. Thank you, God. I believe that you are doing this now. In Jesus' name. Amen."

Miriam looked at her watch. "It's time to see Frank. I'm going in with you, Emily. We'll both pray and thank God for healing him."

Frank didn't open his eyes as they stood side by side at his bed and gently laid their hands on his arm. They prayed, Emily kissed his fingers and they left. The nurses hadn't noticed the second person enter with Emily. And certainly they couldn't know that a Third Person was also in Frank's room.

When the two women came back into the small waiting room, the Jewish man was still there. His head was bowed and his face very pale. He reached out for Miriam's hand and said, "Oh, what you have shown me today! Who are you, that you could carry such a message that would cut through my sorrow like a sword?"

Before Miriam could answer he continued. "Pray for my wife. My Miriam. She may not last the night. It's cancer. I can't lose my Miriam."

Miriam Maxom knelt at his feet and said, "My name is Miriam, too. Do you believe that Jesus is the Son of God?"

"I didn't, but I do now."

"Do you believe that God can heal your wife, in the name of His Son?"

The man nodded again.

"So do I," said Miriam. The man joined Miriam on the floor. Emily put her bag and the hairdresser's book on the chair and knelt with them. Emily and Miriam prayed for the unknown Miriam. "Heal your handmaiden, Lord. So that she may come to know you as her husband now knows. In the name of Jesus. Amen." Miriam finished, and the man said simply, "Thank you, Father. Thank you, Messiah."

He gave Miriam a card with his name on it and asked for her name. She quickly wrote it on a church envelope she had in her purse. She and Emily left. The "spirit-filled" book[2] from the hairdresser remained on the chair. The man dropped his newspaper to the floor and picked it up. The book was the story of another Jewish soul in quest of his Messiah. Another instrument of God's peace, working to accomplish good in all things, so that the glory of the Lord might be shown.

CHAPTER ELEVEN

Shall We Pray?

WHEN MIRIAM returned to the church after dropping Emily at her home, she was still full of the glow she'd felt at the hospital. It was as though she moved and functioned in her usual way, yet not she herself was doing it. "Not I, but Christ," she said aloud. "Oh, how wonderful to have discovered that He is real. That it's all true." She had absolutely no doubt that Frank and Miriam would be healed. She hadn't yet looked at the man's card in her purse and didn't do so now. It was imperative that she check the office to see how the Lord had provided Dr. Mahoney with his session copies. Not *if* he had provided, but *how*.

Dr. Mahoney was gone for the day. The church was empty except for Mr. Walker setting up chairs in the lounge for the meeting of the session. She sat at her desk and read the note stuck in her typewriter.

> The Lord provided Elizabeth Hanlon to prepare my notes.
> Do you think He might also provide a quorum for tonight?
> P.S.: we could use a little peace and good will, too.
>
> A. M.

Miriam laid her head on the desk and rested for a few minutes. Suddenly she felt very tired. She thanked God for using her this afternoon and asked Him to guide the meeting tonight. It was getting late, time for her to go home and prepare her dinner, but she didn't feel hungry. She remembered having put two frozen dinners in the freezer in the church kitchen and decided to fetch those home. She sometimes did this when she stopped at the grocery store on her way to work or at noon. Chicken pot pie would be just right. Once more she dug "the book" out of her desk and decided to leave it on Andrew Mahoney's desk. Let him see how the Lord would provide fully, if he'd only allow Him to do so. She felt that after tonight's meeting he was going to be in need of numerous provisions. This time after having put it on his desk, she walked deliberately out of the room and didn't look back. Now was the time.

In the education building, Miriam turned on a light in the always-dark kitchen. The aroma of something quite delicious came from the vicinity of the stove — was it eggplant parmesan? Wonder who had cooked here this afternoon?

She got her chicken pies out of the freezer and started out, when she heard voices almost at her feet. Miriam jumped. The voices were discussing Miss Maxom, church secretary.

"Sara Ann told me that Phil, the hairdresser, told her that Miss Maxom received the Baptism in the Holy Spirit with all the trimmings!" It was Phoebe, girl reporter and befriender of newspaper editors in time of trouble. Her brother Peter corrected her.

"The Bible doesn't call them 'trimmings,' Phoebe. They are called gifts, charismata — speaking in tongues, gifts of faith, healing, knowledge, etc. Read it to us, Father, from your KJV."

"Yes, do, dear." It was Priscilla who had suddenly developed a craving for more of "the King's English" than she had ever had before. Jeremiah cleared his throat (as always) and started to read I Corinthians 12:1–13. The eggplant parmesan was getting cold but nobody seemed to mind except John Mark. He kept putting his paw in the dish for a sample.

Kneeling down so that she might hear what was said, Miriam heard Jeremiah read the verses and conclude with the thirteenth, "For by one Spirit are we all baptized into one body, whether we be Jews or Gentiles, whether we be bond or free; and have been all made to drink into one Spirit." Now she felt reassured that it also included the Jewish man and his Miriam, for whom she'd prayed today. She tapped discreetly at the cabinet door. The reading stopped. Utter silence greeted her.

"Hello, in there. I'm Miriam, a Christian friend. I'd like to know you so I can thank you for reading those verses. Some of the things you just read about happened to me this afternoon."

With that, the cabinet door swung open and Miriam came face to face with the family of Jeremiah Malachi Mouse. He introduced each member in turn. "My wife, Priscilla. My eldest son, Peter. This is Timothy, Phoebe, John Mark and Baby Mary."

"I'm very pleased to meet you," said Miriam. "I'm the church secretary as you perhaps know. Do know, in fact, since you also know I've received the Baptism in the Holy Spirit. Is your family Charismatic?"

Jeremiah said that he, Peter, Timothy and Phoebe had been baptized and received some of the gifts mentioned in I Corinthians.

"Aren't they just terrific?" Phoebe was so excited.

"Why haven't the rest of you received?" Miriam wanted to know.

"No one has asked me, or said much about it," said Priscilla. "But the minute they do, I'm ready!" She gave her husband a fond look.

"Mary's too young, isn't she?" It was Timothy, the organist, who spoke.

Still kneeling, Miriam smiled and said, "Didn't the Lord Jesus say 'let the children come to me and forbid them not for of such is the kingdom of heaven?' "

"That's right," said Peter. "He didn't specify what age, did he?"

"Count me out," said John Mark. "I don't want any of your creepy religion. You are all too super-Christian to suit me. Uncle Reginald has got the right idea; the less religion the better." Without waiting to partake of the cold eggplant he asked to be excused to go and ride his Mike.

"His what?" inquired Miriam.

"It's a miniature bicycle made especially for mice," Peter told her. "A mouse-bike; a Mike. He's our holdout, can't really understand how we feel about this."

"Well, don't worry," Miriam answered. "He'll come around. Has to. You've got him surrounded!"

Jeremiah left his seat at the head of the mouse table, and found a small stool near where Miriam knelt. He and his two sons pushed it over to the cabinet, so that the secretary might visit them in comfort.

Priscilla felt obliged to invite Miriam to dine with them. Miriam declined with thanks but did accept the offer of a cup of tea. It was really delicious tea, and she'd have been glad of a helping of the eggplant, but she felt sure her appetite would leave little for the mice.

"Does the pastor know you're in residence here?" she inquired of Jeremiah.

The patriarch of the mouse clan assured her that the reverend knew but hadn't as yet discovered their habitat. "Yea and verily, he has laid snares all about us and near the tents of our habitation. We've eluded him, only by the grace of God and the safekeeping of the Holy Spirit."

"I like you," said Miriam. "I'm glad you're here. You're just what this church needs. Perhaps you can help bring our pastor to the Baptism in the Spirit. If ever a man needed to be emptied of his intellectual ideas and filled with spiritual ones, it is he."

"The Lord has told us that Father will be the instrument by which the Reverend Dr. Andrew Pinkham Mahoney comes to receive the Spirit baptism." Peter announced this with a combination of pride and humility. Jeremiah reacted with a combination of joy and irritation. "Why me, Lord? Why me?" Then his face lighted up and he said, "Why not me?"

He glanced at his loving wife and noticed that she was twitching a great deal more than usual. In fact, she appeared to be so nervous that she was wiping her dishes on the blue apron she wore instead of the tea towel. She kept whispering to herself.

"My dearest Priscilla, what are you saying to yourself that you can't say aloud to present company?"

"I'm saying, dear husband, that it's high time you all prayed for me to receive the baptism, as I am about to explode."

Miriam laughed. "Just what I was about to suggest, Mrs. Mouse."

Priscilla took a seat at the end of the long table (which was a spaghetti box tonight) and her family surrounded her.

"Wait," said Priscilla. "Let me hold Baby Mary, and she can also partake of this blessing."

She lifted the small girl mouse from her butter tub/crib, patted her fondly, and cradled her in motherly paws.

Miriam laid a gentle finger upon the wee warm mouse, and her hand lightly on the mother. Timothy, Peter and Phoebe each put paws on their mother, while Jeremiah embraced her with one paw, balancing his trusty KJV in the other. He prayed.

"Dearly beloved, we are gathered here in the sight of God and each other to ask the blessings of Almighty God to fall upon our most precious wife and baby; mindful that John the Baptist said Jesus would baptize in the Holy Spirit. Do you, Priscilla, acknowledge Jesus Christ to be your Lord and Savior?"

"I do — from my earliest days in the cathedral, I have."

"And do you acknowledge Him also for our daughter, Mary Lydia Dorcas, and promise to teach her God's way in all things?"

"Oh, yes!"

"Now, dear Jesus, if there be anything here that is not of thee, please cast it out: all uncleanness, all evil, all unbelief. Baptize these two in your Holy Spirit, and give them each the gifts they may need to serve you more fully. Amen."

By the time they had concluded their fellowship, it was quite dark, and Miriam, clutching her partially thawed chicken pot pies, met the first people arriving for Andrew's meeting of the session. He had arrived sometime earlier, as his car was in his accustomed parking slot already. Her knees began to knock as she pictured him thumbing through the book she'd left on his desk.

"I know it's your battle, Lord. I just supplied a little ammunition. Now I'm not going to worry about it anymore."

All the elders had arrived and were seated, and the pastor hadn't yet put in an appearance. He was already on the premises, they knew, for they had seen his car. Perhaps his watch had stopped. Jim Logan was about to go down the hall and knock at his door, when the minister walked in.

"Sorry to be late, but something came up."

He carried several notebooks and papers in his hand. The meeting got underway. Peter and Jeremiah were hidden on the window ledge behind a blue plaid curtain. The evening was cold, and Jeremiah had a woolen shawl around his shoulders. Peter had thrown an old sweatshirt over his neat blue suit. They had their Bibles and could easily read by the overhead light. Jeremiah's teeth began to chatter half-way through the meeting, and he moved closer to Peter for warmth.

Dr. Mahoney was entertaining a request from Willard Carmichael.

"Dr. Mahoney; fellow session members, ladies and gentlemen." Mr. Carmichael was sometimes formal to the point of boredom. Andrew had come to regard him as the "tattle-tale" of the group. He never knew what surprise Willard had in store for them. He wasn't long in finding out this evening.

"Ladies and gentlemen, we've received a request from a Charismatic Catholic group who wonder if they might use one of our meeting rooms for a Saturday night prayer meeting."

"What's a Charismatic Catholic?" Ellen Onderling, maiden school teacher, wanted to know.

"What's a Charismatic Catholic?" echoed Mildred Hatrick, manageress of a local bank.

Several eyes turned to Jim Logan and Bill Gordon. Apparently they were expected to know.

Jim spoke, after a moment's deliberation. "A Charismatic Catholic — or Baptist or Presbyterian, or one of any denomination — is a Christian who has asked God's Holy Spirit to become active in him, and who believes that the Pentecost of the Acts and the gifts spoken of in I Corinthians are available for Christians today."

"Why would they want to meet here?" someone else asked.

Willard answered, "They tell me that they've outgrown their own meeting rooms and wish to split up into smaller groups. I don't think we want to have anything to do with such groups, do we? Besides, we want to keep the church locked on Saturday nights to discourage prowlers. It's not safe to leave it unlocked. You never know who might wander in."

"I wonder what the Lord will say when He returns and finds the church locked and people gathered outside to pray?" Startled, Jim Logan and Bill Gordon looked at the speaker, Cynthia McGowan, wife of a local doctor. Cynthia had just come onto session to replace Harold Bishop, resigned due to the abortion dilemma. Surely this woman spoke as one who had it together.

She turned to Willard Carmichael and smiled disarmingly. "Mr. Carmichael, I am Charismatic and Presbyterian. I assure you, we are quite harmless, and you'd do well to allow the Catholics to pray in our building. In heaven, it's doubtful if we'll be able to tell one from another!"

A light laugh ran around the room, and Andrew Mahoney had to rap for order. Bill Gordon asked permission to speak.

"I guess it's time you all knew that there are other Charismatics in this church, including my wife and me and the Logans. But you really ought to be careful about coming in contact too often with Charismatics. It's contagious, you know — thank the Lord!"

Andrew thought it time to dispense with this discussion and called for a vote on the Catholic request. It was denied.

"Then," said Jim Logan, "I hope there's no objection if we invite them to share our prayer meeting which takes place in the Upper Room over the kitchen every Tuesday at eight. We got permission for that, you know, before Reverend Hanagan left."

The pastor was becoming intensely irritated at the length of time the present discussion was consuming. He had several important items yet to bring forth. He disposed of the whole lot of Charismatics summarily.

"I suggest that you pray in your Upper Room with whom you please, as long as it's done *decently and in order*. We won't tolerate any misbehavior or sensation-seeking on church property. Is that clear? Now, could I have a motion on that?"

Willard Carmichael made the motion; it carried. Cynthia McGowan moved over to sit between Bill Gordon and Jim Logan. "PTL!" she whispered.

The chairman of the Evangelism and Mission Commission had a proposal from a community prayer group requesting that the church participate in a nationwide Day of Repentance and Prayer.

"A what?" was the general response.

"A National Day of Repentance and Prayer," Mr. Harkness explained. "It's patterned after a similar one declared by Abraham Lincoln during the Civil War. One of our senators has proposed it. It's supposed to make us as a nation more conscious of our individual and collective shortcomings and make us want to do better."

"I'm afraid it comes at the wrong time on the liturgical calendar," was Andrew's remark. "We're about to enter the time of prayer and preparation for Easter, and I can't see that it's needed."

Cynthia McGowan's pink face became a shade pinker, and she nervously smoothed her brown hair back from her forehead. "Dr. Mahoney, I doubt if Jesus will schedule his Second Coming to coincide with the liturgical calendar. I suggest it won't hurt us to over-pray rather than under-pray. Why don't we do it?"

The motion passed, but Dr. Mahoney saw he'd clearly invited another Brutus into his presence. He could hardly wait for the meeting to end so he could start work on Sunday's sermon. Never mind that he already had one prepared. This one would be a stop-press! Now he knew who had put the book on his desk. It had to be Cynthia.

CHAPTER TWELVE

Some of My Best Friends
Are...

🐟 ANDREW MAHONEY spent a restless Saturday
night in the manse. Laying it all to indigestion from two
sausage pizzas, he tossed and tumbled, sleeping little. Then
he dreamed.

He couldn't remember having dreamed since his first year
in seminary. It wasn't the same dream, but the one reminded
him of the other. In the seminary dream he had been holding
a tiger by the tail, being pulled along through a jungle, being
scratched and cut by underbrush and brambles. All the time
he felt that if he let go of the tiger's tail, he'd find his feet on
soft green grass, but he wouldn't let go. He never knew where
the tiger was taking him, but he remembered hanging on for
dear life, feeling that if he let go, the tiger might turn on him,
and it would all be over.

The pizza dream was different. This time he was being
pursued by a mouse. A large white mouse with piercing blue

eyes. They were racing up and down the stairs at Bellview Presbyterian Church. With what he thought to be admirable strategy, Andrew reversed his course and came upon the mouse from the rear, latching neatly onto its tail. Whereupon, the mouse turned round and bit him. Andrew woke up screaming, "Don't bite! Don't bite!"

He took two cups of instant coffee and a cinnamon bun for breakfast and felt a little better. His eyes were bloodshot, and he cut himself while shaving. An evil portent if ever there was one, he thought. He felt a little like he had the morning he'd preached the abortion sermon: almost ready to back out, yet knowing full well he couldn't. He wondered if Bibs Hanlon would be there with her recorder. Why hadn't she shown him the latest issue of *The Bell Tower*? He had a sneaking feeling that the article had turned out to be uncomplimentary after all.

During the short drive to the church, he tried to remember what hymns he'd chosen but couldn't. Carlo Entini had turned surly when he discovered no new music was forthcoming from the budget and might in all likelihood play "Mary Had a Little Lamb" as a prelude. How would the people react if he did? At this point Andrew was beyond caring. Never had he come across a more unbending congregation than this.

In a sort of daze he slid unnoticed into his chair behind the pulpit. "Slunk" was Jeremiah's word for it, as he and his family watched from the balcony. One member of their family was missing. John Mark had left for an early ride on his Mike and hadn't returned in time for services. Priscilla tried hard not to look worried, but she was. The prelude began, soft, sweet, rather like a waltz. They couldn't believe it was the same Entini who customarily pulled all the stops for the opening number.

"Ho, everyone that heareth! What have we here?" Jeremiah inquired of his brood. "Verily, the congregation will be sound asleep before he reaches the last note."

Timothy was able to bring them up to date on the music rebellion, as he often heard Carlo talking to himself while he practiced the organ. He was putting on a pitch for more music and new choir robes, at the same time that the church fathers were cutting his music budget in half.

Carlo, of course, blamed the whole thing on Andrew Mahoney. It proved conclusively what he'd often surmised: red-haired men had no taste in music! Carlo planned to lull the congregation to sleep with the prelude and shake them out of their seats with the postlude. What happened in between was none of his affair. Andrew, when he rose to read the scripture, turned and smiled at Carlo, waving a half-salute with his hand, just to let the organist know that he, Andrew, knew what the score was. And it wasn't Bach!

There was a larger crowd than usual, and this puzzled Andrew. He read from Good News for Modern Man, I Corinthians, chapter 12, verses 1–31. He enumerated the various gifts of the Holy Spirit and then defined the word "Charismatic."

"What is a Charismatic Christian, and are there any such in Bellview Presbyterian Church? A Charismatic Christian, to quote one of our elders, is a Catholic or Baptist or Presbyterian, or one of any denomination who has asked for God's Holy Spirit to become active in him, and who believes that the Pentecost of the Acts and the gifts spoken of in I Corinthians are available for Christians today.

"And yes, Virginia, we have some in Bellview Presbyterian. It's all too obvious that Charismatics place undue emphasis on the spectacular gifts and not enough on the gifts that build up the church.

"I quote from I Corinthians 14:12. 'Since you are eager to

have the gifts of the Spirit, above everything else you must try to make greater use of those which help build up the church.'

"I suggest to you this morning that the gifts which are really needed to build up the church in this place are not the spectacular gifts of speaking in tongues, or miracles or words of knowledge, but the practical gifts given to those people who serve on our committees and boards. Blessed is he who can manage a successful stewardship drive, for without him we would have no funds. Blessed are the teachers, for if they teach not the children, who shall? Blessed are the women who rise up early and bake the cakes and meatloaves for the church dinners; who plan the bazaars and fund-raisers. If these same women were running around speaking in unknown languages how would we understand them?

"For we are all members of the Body of Christ in this church and in the Church universal. I declare to you that the trustee who helps paint the church on Saturday is just as holy as the man who prays in an unknown tongue on Sunday. The man who mows the church lawn is just as Charismatic as the one who prays for a miracle.

"Don't you see, friends, that it's just these spectacular things that divide the church, when above all things we desire unity.

"Let us henceforth resolve to take all our gifts and make them Charismatic. As you know from recent reports, our pledges are far short of the amount anticipated, and we are forced to cut corners everywhere. Mr. Entini could use a part-time, unpaid choir assistant. We won't pay you but we'll classify you as Charismatic! That way you won't feel less than your brethren who speak in tongues. Fair enough?

"The deacons and trustees need helpers to paint the inside of the church and to repair the roof and furnace. All you Charismatic carpenters sign your names at the front door as you leave. And in I Corinthians 12:31 we read, 'Set your hearts then, on the more important gifts. And best of all, of course, is love.'

"If you love your church, if you love your neighbor, *care* what happens. Come forth with your gifts, dedicated to God, for use in building up his kingdom. And what we cannot buy with money we do not have, we will purchase with our Charismatic gifts and our love for one another. We shall leave the Pentecostals and the Charismatics to the Upper Rooms, and we will take care of the church building and grounds. We will type and file, and teach the children ourselves. And since we are in the majority, we shall prevail. It is easy to say Praise the Lord! but difficult to wield a paint brush or pledge an extra five dollars a week.

"When the offering basket is passed we will also pass a 'gift' basket. You will find little yellow slips in the pew racks. On those you may list the gifts you wish to dedicate to God as your Charismatic gifts. Be assured, we will waste no time in allowing you to fulfill that obligation. Yes, Virginia, there are Charismatics and Charismatics. We shall be the working Charismatics who believe that the gift without the giver is bare. Let us give ourselves!"

Andrew's final plea brought the house to complete silence. No one coughed, sneezed or stirred. They were digesting his words, looking at one another. Like children who were promised a pony for Christmas, only to find a rocking horse under the tree, they felt slightly disappointed. What was it exactly he was offering them?

There were fewer than a dozen yellow slips in the gift basket. Many people required time to think this over. Paul Jenkins was heard to remark as he left the sanctuary, "Well, he's succeeded in telling me a lot about something I had no desire to know. I paint all day for a living. I'm darned if I'll also paint all night or on the weekend just to be called a Charismatic!"

Carol Gordon told her husband, "I'm sick. Just sick. If anybody here had the remotest desire to experience the abundance of God's spiritual gifts, he's successfully bollixed it. Closed the door to further inquiry, you might say."

Sue Logan asked them, "What do we do now?"

Jim, her husband, answered, "We will pray. There's no defense against a weapon like that."

Bill Gordon felt at least it was all out in the open. "Now we won't have to meet in secret. We'll invite our Catholic and Baptist friends and lay such a covering of prayer on him and the whole church that soon he won't know what hit him. It's like we're in the same ballgame but on different teams. Too bad."

During the ensuing weeks a slow dribble of yellow slips came into the church office. Miriam received them, categorized them and turned the whole thing over to Dr. Mahoney. His aides immediately began calling volunteers to paint, hammer and repair. Not content with that, the new minister instituted a Lenten program of study for the committees and boards and in the adult education classes about the matter of the gifts.

Soon every meeting began with the reading of Corinthians, Ephesians and the Acts. People were beginning to be interested. Some were doing research. The Gordons, Logans and Cynthia McGowan found that they were invited to speak to various groups within the church by interested members. Dr. Mahoney never seemed to be present at these particular meetings, however. The little group of Charismatics continued to meet in the Upper Room with their counterparts from other churches in town.

Miriam Maxom had become a regular attendant along

with Emily Ardmore, who had received the Baptism in the
Holy Spirit. Now that her Frank was home she was able to
get out in the evening some. Monica was only too glad to
stay with her father. It was now too late for her to have an
abortion. She discussed the matter fully with Miriam and her
parents and decided to place her baby for adoption after its
birth.

Meanwhile, she was taking courses at the technical school
which would allow her to graduate in June. She and her
father had become very close as she read to him and helped
her mother about the house. It was Emily whose life had
changed the most since her husband's miraculous recovery.

One Tuesday afternoon, just before Miriam was about to
leave the church office, she received a telephone call from the
office of a large law firm in a neighboring town. Thinking it
had to do with Harold Bishop's suit against the church she
quickly grabbed the file from the closet before answering
further.

"Miss Maxom?"

"This is Miss Maxom speaking. May I help you?"

"I'm not sure you'll remember me, but I'm the man whose
wife you prayed for in the hospital last month. I wanted to
call you sooner but lacked the courage, I guess. Because, of
course, I doubted the outcome of your prayer."

Miriam was holding her breath. All the time the man was
talking, she was praying silently, "Thank you, Lord, for
answering that prayer. I know you did. Thank you, God."

"The doctors say it was the most astounding recovery they
ever experienced. The tumor on Miriam's kidney began to
shrink. The fluid cleared from her lungs and she started
intravenous feedings again. Two weeks later she was able to
sit up in bed, and tomorrow I'm bringing her home. Praise
the Lord for his goodness!"

He invited Miriam to come and visit them and to bring some books for them to read. "I call myself a Christian now, but I want to make it official. Will you tell me all the things I need to do?"

Miriam laughed and cried and laughed some more. She hung up the phone and knelt down beside her desk to thank God for healing this woman. While she was praying, Tom Packney walked in with his vacuum cleaner.

Tom felt somewhat embarrassed to come upon "Miss Maximum" in an attitude of prayer in the church office. As long as he'd been working at BPC, he'd never seen anybody kneeling to pray, even in the sanctuary. He didn't quite know what to do or say.

"Amen," said Miss Maxom.

"Are you okay, Miss M.?" Tom asked.

Still half laughing and half crying, Miriam rose and grabbed Tom and hugged him. That's twice she's hugged me, thought Tom, am I so irresistible?

"What's the matter, Miss Maxom?"

"Sit down, Tom. Unplug your sweeper. I have something to tell you." And that's how it came about that Tom Packney met his first live Charismatic.

"So you're what the Padre was preaching about the other Sunday. I never heard of anything like that before."

"Well, my friend, you've heard of it now, and let me tell you that the Charismatic renewal that's sweeping this country is uprooting old prejudices, old feelings and ideas, and making new Christians of us all. You ought to learn more about it, Tom." She invited him to come to the prayer meeting that evening.

"Aw, I don't know about that, Miss M. It's pretty hard for teen-agers to pray in a crowd. I don't think I'd fit in. But I might sometime," he hastened to assure her, as he really did hate to disappoint Miss Maxom. She had gotten to be one of his main supports and allies. He shoved off down the hall with his sweeper, deciding to do the library first.

"Now what in the world are these books doing on the floor?" He stooped to pick up some books that were half off the bottom shelf. Almost as if someone had started to read them and left quickly. He looked at the titles: *"The Holy Spirit and You"* [3] by Dennis and Rita Bennett, *"Nine O'Clock in the Morning"* [4] by Dennis Bennett and a third book, with a slice of half-eaten Swiss cheese sticking between the pages, was *"They Speak with Other Tongues"* [5] by John Sherrill. He stopped the vacuum cleaner and started thumbing through them. He forgot to finish his cleaning; forgot to go home to supper. It had gotten dark, so he switched on the light and read some more. He saw that it was eight p.m.

"Well, since I'm this late I might as well see what Miss Maxom's friends are doing in the Upper Room. These books are like *wow!*"

And so it came to pass that Tom Packney, custodian's helper, entered a Charismatic prayer meeting and came out a different person. He knew several of the young people who were there, and that helped to give him courage to ask for their prayers.

"This stuff's dynamite!" he told Miss Maxom, as she showed him where it all came from in the Bible. "I feel like Matthew, Mark, Luke and John all rolled into one!"

The next day at independent study he took his Bible along to look up all the verses that told about the Holy Spirit baptism. Bibs found him sitting on the floor in the resource center absorbed in his reading.

"So the Padre's got you hooked?" was her caustic comment.

"Heck no, Bibs, it's not the Padre. I never learned about this from him. Miss Maxom told me about it. She says it's all

over town. I went last night to their prayer meeting and got
baptized in the Holy Spirit and spoke in the prettiest words
you ever heard!"

"Come on, Tom, stop the fooling. You're just saying that
on account of the story I did on the Padre. You did get mad,
after all."

"No, actually I didn't. He got mad, but I didn't. I thought
it was good, how you told all about his upbringing: 'astrin-
gent', wasn't it?"

"*Stringent*, Tom. And antiseptic. He has a disinfected
mind that won't allow the germ of emotion to enter. I just
said he was making a farce of the Charismatic renewal. I've
studied all about that. My English II teacher is Charismatic,
and she lent me some of her books. I like the idea. It's pretty
potent — but it's not for me. But for an altogether different
reason than Dr. Mahoney's."

"You can come with me Tuesday night if you want to,
Bibs. And see for yourself."

"No thanks."

This was Friday. Tuesday after school Bibs Hanlon drove
by Tom's house on her way home. She left a note in the
door.

"Tom, if you're going to the PM tonight, I might go along.
Want to pick me up?

Bibs"

CHAPTER THIRTEEN

A New Song

PEOPLE BEGAN arriving early for the Tuesday night prayer meeting, and soon the small upstairs room was filled to overflowing, with several young people sitting on the steps outside the door. Before they started singing, Jim Logan counted thirty-four people, and he heard others come up and lean against the wall outside the room. The Upper Room was bulging as never before. Added to the body warmth was the excessive heat from the furnace directly below, and in spite of the winter weather, someone finally had to open the windows. Unknown to the singers and those who were praising God, the music was clearly audible in the parking lot and in the church yard below.

Andrew Mahoney arrived to check some reference books in the church library. Reginald Rat arrived to visit his old friend, Jeremiah. They walked up the path together from the parking lot, Reggie stepping carefully in the minister's footprints outlined in the light layer of snow that had fallen

during the morning. Both were brought up short by a rousing "Amen! Praise the Lord!" from the window above. Reginald had to apply his brakes to keep from plowing into the minister. If Andrew had stepped backwards Reggie would have been done for. He cautiously inched backwards from the minister's oversize footsteps. Then they heard the heavenly chorus.

Like a musical fountain the voices rose, fell and rose again in a blending of unknown tongues and unknown songs. Neither the Reverend nor the Rat had ever heard the like before. Reggie opened his mouth in astonishment, his pipe falling unnoticed into the snow. "By jing," he said aloud, "I'd better check this out with Jeremiah. He'll know what this is all about. Probably them sciatic Christians."

As naturally as if he were answering a fellow preacher from the local ministerium, Andrew replied. "Don't think you'll find this in Jeremiah. Don't think you'll find it in the Book of Common Worship, either. The Charismatics are in reality the chasm-atics, busy building little chasms between Christians. *Hellelujah!*"

"I thought it was '*Hall*elujah' ", Reginald said, backing off into the shadow, not really desiring a confrontation with the Reverend but unable to restrain himself from offering a correction.

"Well, you thought wrong. It's *Hell*elujah!" Andrew said, stooping to pick up a very small brown pipe resting lightly in the powdery snow. Still warm, he noted. "That means the mice are at it again," he stated flatly.

Reginald decided not to keep "at it", but to return to his bachelor pad. He didn't feel up to a verbal sparring bout with Jeremiah after all. Somehow the bitterness and frustration in the young minister's voice had a very depressing effect upon the champion grumbler from the Hardware Store. He decided to consult Jeremiah the prophet not Jeremiah the mouse. Instead of turning on the one small electric light in the stockroom of the store, Reggie lit a candle and thrust it into an empty pickle jar. He turned to Jeremiah 17:12 and read two verses, blew out the candle and went to bed.

Andrew Mahoney closed the door of his study, locked it carefully and drew the curtains, as if in so doing he might shut out all sounds of the prayer meeting. He was successful. He reached for his trusty RSV, then on an impulse opened the Living Bible to Jeremiah 17:12, read two verses once, read them again and sat with the Bible open before him for almost an hour. He had read: "But our refuge is your throne, eternal and glorious. O Lord, the Hope of Israel, all who turn away from you shall be disgraced and shamed; they are registered for earth and not for glory, for they have forsaken the Lord, the Fountain of Living Waters. Lord, you alone can heal me, you alone can save, and my praises are for you alone."

An odd situation began to prevail at Bellview Presbyterian Church. Andrew preached more and more on the Book of Acts, I Corinthians and Ephesians. The people didn't know what to believe. Some completely turned off the whole thing; others had their appetites whetted to hear more and set about doing so but at other churches.

Home Bible studies started up and the Upper Room prayer meeting grew steadily larger. Perhaps a dozen people out of the congregation had come for inquiry and stayed for the baptism and the blessing, for the outpouring of the Holy Spirit. A touch of leaven, a bit of yeast began to work quietly but persistently in the boards and committees that met regularly.

Andrew heard rumors, annoying and disquieting, but he was convinced that his duty lay in presenting the gifts of the Spirit in such a manner as to offend no one; desiring that all the Christians in this particular Body of Christ be equal. The flamboyant, the spectacular, he eschewed heartily. He didn't hear the mice, but he heard people talking in the halls and in the meeting rooms. They broke off abruptly as he joined them. Several families left the church; some because they couldn't stand the constant wrangling and others because they had found their answer in the atmosphere of churches with a Pentecostal flavor. Harold Bishop won his suit to regain his pledge money, while Andrew Mahoney's budget sank lower and lower. So did his prospects.

Things started happening to him that seemed like a carefully planned conspiracy. He began to feel that God had it in for him. The plagues descended shortly after Easter.

Coming home late from a session meeting one night, he ran out of gas on a side street a half-mile from the manse. It was futile to try to locate an open station at midnight, so he locked the car and walked home. The next morning it was missing.

Police in Newark, New Jersey discovered it abandoned near the railroad station. How it got there on an empty tank, no one surmised.

Two uncommonly warm days followed after Easter and Andrew turned the heat back very low. He enjoyed a "cool" sleep. The next afternoon he went out of town to a synod meeting and left the heat so low that the pipes in the manse bathroom froze and burst when the temperature dropped unexpectedly. Water flowed out of the bathroom and into the kitchen, den and dining room. A Charismatic carpenter and a Charismatic plumber from his congregation came to the rescue.

Three days later he was just pulling away from a stop sign

when he was hit broadside by a delivery truck from a local liquor store. Broken bottles and pungent liquid flowed in the streets of Bellview. His shoes smelled of Scotch where he stepped in the liquor and his car was out of commission for two weeks.

He stopped blaming God and began to blame it all on the mice. Poor Mr. Walters, the elderly custodian, was again set to baiting traps with cheese. Additional traps were added and a youthful member of the kindergarten choir caught the toe of her shoe in one as she climbed the stairs to the choir loft one April Sunday. The choir mothers, tired of dodging traps in the music room and on the stairs, went on strike until the traps were removed. Carlo Entini, wrathful that no money was allotted for new music, went on strike until the minister was removed. In the end, a peacemaking committee called on the organist and effected his return, on the written guarantee that the traps would be removed. Mr. Walters made a valiant effort to locate and remove them all. But Mr. Walters, poor of sight, missed a few.

Andrew made another appointment at the doctor's office. He carried his empty pill bottle in his hand.

Dr. Abernathy wasn't really too pleased to see his patient, Dr. Mahoney. If it were possible to couch his true diagnosis in laymen's terms, he'd have said that the new minister had a screw loose. Anyway, he had an innate mistrust of clergymen, dating back to his wedding day. Eleanor, his bride, was the original women's libber, for she had persuaded the elderly minister to have that part of the marriage vows, "love, honor and obey," repeated by only one party: the groom. Thus it was that Irving J. B. Abernathy, in 1950, was promising to obey his wife. She'd never let him forget it, and he'd never forgiven the long-dead Mr. Livingstone. Irving J. B. Abernathy faced his patient, who was once more seated on the paper-covered table, wrapped in a sheet.

"Dr. Mahoney, I can't believe that you're still having that same trouble. Is it the voices again?"

"Well, yes and no. I mean yes I still hear the voices but no, that's not the trouble. I know who they are now."

"Who they are? Well, who are they?"

"Mice. Churchmice. We seem to have a whole family of them, and they have friends and relatives scattered all through the neighborhood. It wouldn't surprise me if you had some here in your offices."

"Dr. Mahoney, rest assured we do not have mice in these offices. But if we did, I'd call an exterminator and have done with them. But anyway, with a church the size of yours, I should think a few tiny squeaks would scarcely be heard. You must have very good ears indeed."

While Dr. Abernathy was speaking, he was taking Andrew's pulse, his temperature, checking his heart and blood pressure. When the thermometer was out of his mouth, Andrew hastened to explain.

"It isn't your simple, little everyday squeaks, Doctor. That I could hack. It's when they talk or sing or pray that I find them most unnerving. Now I have a knot in my stomach."

Not pausing in stride, not blinking an eyelash, Dr. Abernathy set immediately to examining his patient's eyes, ears and head.

"Have you had a fall recently?"

"No."

"Are there any incidents of schizophrenia or manic depression in your family?"

Andrew's cheeks became almost as red as his hair.

"Now, see here, Dr. Abernathy. I'll have you know I'm as sane as the next man, and I'll thank you to keep your schizophrenia to yourself!" He started to throw off the sheet then clutched it desperately as Miss Keegan, the brunette nurse, entered the room.

"See me in my office when you're dressed," the doctor called after the fleeing minister. Andrew carefully dressed and zipped, before entering the doctor's private office. He sat warily across from the portly physician.

"Dr. Mahoney, you are a fine healthy specimen of manhood. With any luck you'll live a good long life. *But*, if I were you I'd seriously consider giving up the ministry and finding another field of endeavor. Obviously the manifold problems in today's religious establishment are too much for you. Why don't you return to the academic world?"

"Because," said Andrew, "I feel *called* to be right here in this church, right now!"

"Very well. Here's a prescription that will settle your stomach and a renewal of your tranquilizer prescription. Also here are names of two prominent and reliable psychiatrists. You'd do well to consult one of them before you have a breakdown."

Andrew thanked him, took the prescriptions, and started for the door. Dr. Abernathy called after him. "And you might try an exterminator."

As soon as Andrew walked out the door, the doctor consulted a desk directory and dialed a number.

"Jim? Irv Abernathy here. Your new minister just left my office. He's in a deal of trouble and you ought to see if you can help him. This is the second time he's been here complaining that he hears mice talking and singing in the church."

The doctor wasn't prepared for the burst of laughter that greeted his announcement. "Well, Praise the Lord! He finally heard them. Don't worry about it, Doc. He's okay. As soon as he gets the message from the little mice, everything will be fine. Thanks a lot. See you at the golf club Saturday."

"Miss Keegan!" The doctor pushed the intercom button.
"Yes, Dr. Abernathy?"

"Cancel my next two appointments. I've got to get out of here early. Like now. I'll be back in the morning." He grabbed his golf jacket and cap and threw his white coat on a chair. "It's those dratted Presbyterians who run amuck every time! That dratted Livingstone was one, and they haven't changed since!"

With Andrew's renewed assault on the Charismatics, he noticed that the church attendance was picking up. The regular members they lost were more than made up by strangers who kept popping in. A large group of young people, friends and followers of Bibs Hanlon and Tom Packney, were seated every Sunday on the first four pews of the right-hand side of the church. Bibs had her ever-present tape recorder.

He had never forgiven her for the sour article she'd written as a follow-up on his abortion sermon. He often told himself, "Paul had his thorn in the flesh, and I have Bibs Hanlon." She wasn't even a member of the church; he didn't know *what* she was. What she was (now) was a Charismatic Presbyterian from across town. She, along with Tom and several of their friends, had taken to the joy and the praise of the enriched life in the Holy Spirit like a duck takes to water.

Bibs had become almost an authority on the subject, from having had Miss Tomlins, a Charismatic English teacher, all year. Every Friday night some thirty or forty seniors, juniors and sophomores met in the rec room at Bib's home for Bible study and instruction on "how to share your faith." Miss Tomlins came and frequently Miss Maxom, accompanied by the new minister from the Baptist Church across the street from BPC. A shy, clean-cut man, exactly Miss Maxom's age, he had declared early that he was a Charismatic in search of kindred spirits. Bibs and Tom sensed romance as well as joy in the air, and they were delighted. Tom was delighted to be in the same room with Bibs and to know that at last they had something in common: the uncommon joy of an abundant life in the Holy Spirit.

"Where's this been all the time?" Tom asked Miss Maxom. "My folks had me baptized when I was twelve, but I never heard of the Holy Spirit until now!"

Miriam explained to Tom that God's Holy Spirit had never really been away since Pentecost. The same power and manifestations of the Spirit that were given the apostles and early Christians could be had by believing Christians today just for the asking.

"That's what's needed, Tom — the asking. Most of us didn't ask because we didn't know, and we didn't know because no one told us. People who were afraid of emotion in religion didn't stress it and some people simply thought it wasn't applicable in modern times."

"It makes the whole thing real to me, Miss M. Like, I never was sure that God was anyplace but way up there somewhere, and He probably couldn't be bothered about a guy like me. But now — wow! It's like getting a personal letter from God! With my name on it!"

Miriam smiled at Tom across the desk in the office.

"You put that well, Tom. That's really what's meant by accepting Christ as your personal Savior; believing that He means you, Tom Packney, can have eternal life!"

"Not only eternal but now! You know, Miss M., if every kid who'll be going away to college had something like this to zero in on, what a difference it would make! I've stopped shifting around and settled on where I want to go and what I want to study, because Somebody helped me make up my mind, and it wasn't Mom and Dad. They don't understand what I'm talking about. And boy, I sure do wish the Padre could dig this."

The Padre never knew exactly how many people were praying for that very thing. As it was, everytime he stood in the pulpit he felt like a man in a sinking ship. He wanted to put on a life preserver. The knot in his stomach grew larger and he gave up pizza altogether.

Lately he'd noticed a different mouse voice in his study, and this one he could never find though he carefully searched the closets and drawers. It sounded somewhat like a teen-age mouse whose voice was changing — if there was such a creature.

There was. It was John Mark, reluctant, recalcitrant son of Jeremiah Malachi Mouse, casing the minister's study, pursuant to a plan he'd formulated months before but hadn't the courage to put into action. With the steady but sure uptrend of "religiosity" in his own family and among his acquaintances at the Mousecoteque he frequented, he'd just about had it. Somehow he knew it wasn't the minister's fault; if anything he should have been sympathetic to Andrew's plight. But he wasn't; in essence, it was Andrew blaming the mice for his misfortunes and John Mark blaming Andrew for the super-Christians he felt his family had become.

What's more, he felt alienated because he couldn't share their joy and pleasure in discussing the Bible and in their prayers and songs. He rode his Mike farther away from church, refused to wheel Baby Mary in her carriage and stayed longer at the Mousecoteque in the Corner Drug Store. He could no longer count on Phoebe to help him heckle the minister. He was more disobedient than he'd ever been to Priscilla and it irritated him to hear his mother praying for him. Everytime Timothy or Peter attempted to talk to him, he ran away. Some days he didn't even put in an appearance for lessons or meals, a fact duly noted by his Father.

"Young man, your presence is hereby requested at nine o'clock Saturday morning in the backyard under the third oak tree. It behooveth thee to be on time, my son!"

John Mark debated leaving home entirely, but he did rather hate to leave his mother and her delicious cooking. Where would he ever be likely to find turnip pie made as his mother made it? He decided to stick it out awhile longer; besides, he still had a few days before Saturday. Meanwhile, he busied himself with letting the air out of the minister's tires every day. The two front tires one day, the two rear tires the next. The gas station across the street was beginning to be more than a little annoyed to find an air customer lined up with the gas customers every morning. Andrew took to buying his gas in two-gallon lots. He purchased a bicycle pump which he kept in his car at all times. He earnestly desired to install mousetraps on his automobile tires but couldn't face the looks he was certain would follow him. He decided to brazen it out, for he knew the mouse days were numbered. Hadn't he dialed the number himself? 316-8080.

"Good morning. Termite and Rodent Control."

"Ma'm, this is Reverend Andrew Mahoney of the Bellview Presbyterian Church. Would you please have an exterminator out here as soon as possible? We seem to be infested with mice."

"Mice?" The operator's voice had rather a shrill squeak itself, or else she was chewing gum.

"Yes, mice."

"What kind of mice?"

"What kinds are there? We've got big ones, little ones, an occasional rat, but I don't know what *kind* they are. Is it important?"

"Oh, yes, it's important. But I never heard of anyone wanting to get rid of churchmice. They're supposed to be kind of, you know, good luck, don't you think?"

"Well, you've heard of it now, and they're not good luck. They're bad luck, and I want them out. OUT! Now, will you take the order or not?"

"Do you have an authorization from your Board of Trustees to have the work done? Could you give me an authorization number, sir?"

"My word, I never heard of such a complicated procedure just to have an exterminator call. To whom am I speaking, may I ask?"

"Miss Lull — ugh — ogan —"

"Miss Ogan, I'll have an authorization number for you first thing tomorrow morning. If I don't call somebody else meanwhile!" For heaven's sake, you'd think she was working for the mice, Andrew thought as he slammed the receiver down.

Miss Jennifer Logan, bright as a button, dialed her father immediately after her caller hung up. "Dad, the minister just called. He wants the mice exterminated!"

Jim Logan assured her that there was nothing to worry about. "This is prayer meeting night and some of the mice usually show up. We'll pass the word around and have them clear out when your boss shows up. Don't worry about it, honey. And thanks for thinking of the little creatures."

CHAPTER FOURTEEN

The Prophecy of
Jeremiah—Retold

ANDREW MAHONEY dropped his sermons on the Charismatic aspect of Christianity in favor of a series based on the book of Jeremiah. Suddenly he'd become fascinated with the prophecies he found there. Perhaps it was time to hit the parishioners with a bit of old-fashioned sin. Nothing else seemed to be working. Pledges were still down; the church roll was depleted, yet each Sunday he saw a few new faces in the pews. It was hard for Andrew to understand. Who were they and why didn't they join the church? He checked each pew card carefully for prospective members.

Still drawn to Chapter 17, he used the first verse as his subject. "My people sin as though commanded to, as though their evil were laws chiseled with an iron pen or diamond point upon their stony hearts or on the corners of their altars." With that as a background, he titled his sermon, "Thou Shalt Sin!" The sermon, as he wrote it, moved smoothly from the beginning, and he built his ending around verses twelve through fourteen:

"They have forsaken the Lord, the Fountain of living waters. Lord you alone can heal me, you alone can save, and my praises are for you alone."

Miriam Maxom, typing his sermon on Thursday, smiled when she came to the part about the "Fountain of living waters." She decided to underline it so that he might perhaps *stress* it a little bit. He's singing the right words, she thought, but just a little off-key. If he only would partake of the Living Waters, oh, what a change would come over this church! She underlined it twice.

Several people told him on the way out of church that they'd enjoyed his sermon. I knew it, thought Andrew, sin gets them every time. He was looking over the visitors cards that had been left in the pew.

"What church is this, the Grace of God Church on Milligan Road? And why are there so many visitors lately from there?"

Jim Logan answered, "That's one of the Pentecostal churches in the area. I think they've come to check out your sermons on the Charisma." And so have some of the Methodists and the Baptists and the Lutherans, he added under his breath.

Andrew Mahoney was incensed. "Well, I hope they don't expect to find anything here that suits them! Besides, I'm beginning another series, as you perhaps noted this morning." He was already looking forward, thinking ahead to next week's sermon.

So was the editor of *The Bell Tower*. The following Wednesday Bibs Hanlon published her first "sermonette," taking as her text, Jeremiah 2:11–13.

"And yet my people have given up their glorious God for

silly idols! The heavens are shocked at such a thing and shrink back in horror and dismay. For my people have done two evil things: They have forsaken me, the Fountain of Life-giving Water; and they have built for themselves broken cisterns that can't hold water!" The title of her by-lined article was "Broken Cisterns." She took him apart verse by verse, line by line.

I have listened every Sunday for weeks as the Reverend Andrew Pinkham Mahoney of the Bellview Presbyterian Church has done his utmost to substitute 'silly idols for a glorious God.' He has downgraded and belittled the Charismatic gifts that God is pouring out in abundance on many people in the community, after the same manner as happened in the original Pentecost.

It's happening in Bellview? Believe it! People in this town, young and old and in-between, are feeling the rise and swell of waves of Living Waters which inundate their old lives and fling them back upon the sand as New Lives. Christians from every denomination in this town gather for prayer meetings where they have one common purpose: to Praise the Lord! To glorify the Almighty, the King of Creation! To lift up His Son, Jesus Christ, as Redeemer and Savior. These are people who have asked to be renewed and filled with God's Holy Spirit so that He may work through them in the lives of earthly men.

Is it helping? Believe it! We have seen answered prayer for healings, miraculous healings; faith is renewed; families are united and strengthened, and love and joy are busting out all over! I don't know how it's affecting other ministers in town, but it's not too pleasing to the Rev. Dr. APM. He would have them offer their idols of human talent, human ambition, money and effort to their Maker, rather than accept His wondrous gifts of supernatural languages, supernatural wisdom, knowledge and healing.

He encourages them, even offers the blueprint so that they

may build Broken Cisterns in which to store their Living Water. It won't *hold* water, my friend. If you are thirsty for the Water that leaves you quenched forever, you will need a better vessel than a *broken cistern.* The vessel you must offer Him for filling is nothing less than yourself! And all the people said Amen!

PS: This week he switched to sin."

When Tom came to vacuum the downstairs offices, he quietly slipped into the Padre's office and laid a copy of the paper on his desk. He hadn't the nerve to give it to him in person. Tom felt that Bibs had gone too far this time. She wasn't a preacher. She wouldn't even be an editor this time next week, probably. He could just imagine the irate parents, the civil rights members, the agnostics and the atheists who would descend upon her en masse. Poor Bibs — he wondered if she'd be allowed to graduate. You never knew how far some people would take a thing like this. The Supreme Court, maybe? He prepared a defense for her as he vacuumed.

Tom didn't notice Dr. Mahoney enter his office. He didn't see him leave, face a bright shade of red, the newspaper rolled into a tight cylinder. Miss Maxom saw and shivered. But only for a second, then she remembered to thank the Lord for the whole thing, and immediately felt it would be all right.

For Andrew, it was the straw that broke the back of the camel. He was stopped by the Safety Patrol policeman for going 45 in a 25 mph zone enroute to Bellview High School. He accepted the ticket with pleasure, counting it not too high a price to pay to finally rid himself of his thorn in the flesh. This girl must go! go! go! He was mentally preparing his libel suit as he drove into the parking lot at the school.

The mice were gathered for lunch around an upturned cherry carton, freshly laid with a white linen napkin. Small bowls of carrot soup and crackers were set at each plate. Freshly sliced cheddar cheese in minute wedges, bits of sliced apple and hot gingerbread completed their noon meal. Everyone was present, even John Mark. This was the first time in days that the mouse clan had gathered at noon to relax and enjoy each other's company. It was their chance to be mice among mice. They felt safe and secure here. After his father had concluded the noon Bible reading, Peter read from *The Bell Tower.*

"This looks like the ninth round for him," Phoebe spoke up. "I'm not even sure he'll make it out of his corner, when the bell rings. I'm counting him out now!"

"Phoebe!" Priscilla took her daughter to task for such unladylike manners. "Where did you pick up that kind of talk?"

"We had to watch the end of the prizefight last night while waiting for Oral Roberts to come on TV."

"Oh, well, if it was Oral Roberts," Priscilla felt reassured. "Speaking of Oral Roberts, has anyone seen Reginald lately?"

Her spouse didn't get the connection. "Why would Oral Roberts make you think of Reginald? And no, I haven't seen him lately."

"Poor Reggie is so in need of healing — if he could just get to somebody like Oral Roberts or Kathryn Kuhlman, perhaps he could be helped."

"Mother," Peter's whiskers twitched as he talked, and his square gold-rimmed spectacles bounced up and down on his nose. "Mother, I've been reading a lot in the Bible about how Jesus healed the people who came to him with all kinds of diseases and infirmities. Why don't we start praying now that the Lord will direct Uncle Reggie to come and ask for healing?"

"Why can't we just go to him and lay hands on him and pray for him?" Timothy, the organist, wanted to know.

"Dear wife and sons, we are cautioned in the scriptures, I Timothy 5:22, to lay hands suddenly on no man. It seemeth right and proper as done in the Holy Writ. Jesus healed all those who *came and asked* or *were brought* by faithful friends. No, we can't gang up on Reggie. We must wait upon the Lord."

"Could we maybe hurry things up a bit by pushing him into a trap?" John Mark blurted out, knowing at once he shouldn't have said it.

Five pairs of bright mouse eyes turned fiercely upon their son and brother.

"Bite your tongue!" said Phoebe.

"Thou art snared with the words of thy mouth," quoted his father, Proverb-ially.

Timothy looked disgusted. Peter bowed his head as if to ask forgiveness for his wayward sibling. Baby Mary stopped drinking her bottle and burped.

"I can't believe you meant to say that, dear," was his mother's assurance to him.

Large tears gathered in John Mark's eyes and dripped into his gingerbread. He wasn't hungry anymore, so he got up and left the table after mumbling a hasty "excuse me."

"Let us pray," said Jeremiah.

"Dear Lord of all, our hearts are troubled by the prodigal in our bosom. He giveth us much concern. Because you loved your Son so much, we know you understand how we love young John. Touch him with your loving hand and keep him safe, until he can come willingly into your kingdom. We give you thanks for all of these, our children. And we thanketh thee also for the Reverend Mahoney, who is somebody's son and our prodigal pastor. We love him, too. All praise to thee, Lord Jesus, in whose name we pray. Amen."

John Mark wheeled his Mike out of the storage closet in the hall and rode off toward the town playground nearby. When he returned to the church he was balancing a small package on his handlebars. He resolved to pay off the minister tonight before leaving home tomorrow. He'd decided to stow away on the first ship he could find. Maybe he'd go to Turkey. Failing that, he knew he could always get a bus to Hackensack.

He laid his package in a bush near the kitchen entrance. When it was dark, he meant to set out on his mission. He sat on the package underneath the bush until he saw the minister's car return to church and leave again just before dark. He heard his mother call him several times to come to supper but he paid no heed. Better a clean break, he thought, than to go in and eat her tuna soufflé and then leave. That would be ungrateful!

Andrew's visit to the principal and vice-principal at Bellview High School lasted over an hour and a half. Dr. Heggel, the principal, had very little to say in the matter, while Ms. Prather, the vice-principal, scarcely stopped talking the whole time. She was on Andrew's side from start to finish, she assured him. How she contrived to make this seem less than a blessing Andrew was not quite sure. But she did. He hated to be judgmental, but thin-faced, sharp-featured, skinny women always made him distrustful.

They had, she hastened to say, summoned Miss Hanlon, her parents, the PTA president and the newspaper advisor to meet with them early the next morning. Dr. Mahoney was also invited, but they felt it was important to grant him this hurried interview as he had only just this afternoon read the issue. Ms. Prather held up a sheaf of letters, at least they looked like letters, which she said ran three to one against Miss Hanlon's right to print such an article. She ticked off the groups who had objected: the local rabbi, a civil rights group, a prominent agnostic and several ministers from the city-wide ministerial council. One pastor wrote: "Such an article tends to lump all Protestant churches in the Charismatic group, and this, oh pray believe us, is not the case!"

"It's curious, though," Dr. Heggel remarked, "how many students dropped notes in the office mailbox supporting Miss Hanlon's position. Considering the paper has been out only two days, it's surprising how fast the news got around."

"I don't really care how many students support Miss Hanlon or how many ministers and rabbis support me," Andrew stated flatly. "I care very much that Miss Hanlon has taken me as her target-for-tonight on three separate occasions. I refuse to be made an object of ridicule by an upstart, would-be newspaper editor. At the moment I'm seriously inclined to bring suit!"

"You certainly have every right to do so!" agreed Ms. Prather. "Every right!"

Dr. Heggel emptied his oil can on the troubled waters. "Quite likely Miss Hanlon would agree to a public apology, Dr. Mahoney; and she will no doubt be censored by the newspaper guild. Perhaps she'll also be relieved of her editorship for the final issues of *The Bell Tower*."

Ms. Prather wasn't satisfied. "But Dr. Heggel, in all honesty, can we expect Dr. Mahoney, a man of the cloth, to be satisfied with a mere apology? Clearly Miss Hanlon has violated all the principles of objective newspaper writing, and justice must be done."

"Unless, of course, it was an editorial," Andrew mused, half to himself. "They have more leeway in an editorial, don't they?"

"Dr. Mahoney, what are you saying!" Ms. Prather was aghast to think he might be abandoning his own case. Andrew felt obliged to defend himself to the counsel for the defense. All of a sudden he was tired of the whole mess — tired of Bellview, tired of preaching to people who didn't want to be preached to, tired of everything. He thanked the two officials for their time and said he might return tomorrow morning.

On his way back to church, Andrew stopped for gas (and air) and from the service station made a call to Dr. Heggel.

"Dr. Heggel, this is Andrew Mahoney. I'm calling off my dogs. Don't let Miss Hanlon get in trouble over this. Give her a break. Let's say no more about it."

"You're sure that's what you wish to do?"

"Yes, sir, that's what I'd like."

"Well, thank you very much, Dr. Mahoney. For my money, you've just given a beautiful demonstration of cheek-turning. I admire that. Maybe I'll be over to hear you next week!"

"You do that," Andrew laughed. He laughed again as he pictured Ms. Prather's face when she heard he had abandoned his suit.

Andrew decided not to return to the church immediately. Instead, he would take a short ride in the nearby mountains, after stopping at Inverness Hospital to call on one of his parishioners.

Jacob Watson, suffering from stomach ulcers, was a bachelor in his late seventies. Tight-fisted, he was nevertheless about to name BPC as beneficiary of his sizable estate. He had hardly said a kind word to Andrew in the past five months, and Andrew dreaded walking into his room. At first he thought Jacob was asleep, he lay smiling so peacefully. Then he thought he was dead. Andrew's legs grew weak.

Jacob opened his eyes. "Ah, Mahoney, come in, boy. Thought you weren't coming. Been in a week, you know. Only people been in were Miss Maxom and Mrs. Ardmore — the one with the pregnant daughter."

Andrew inquired how Mr. Watson felt and offered to pray with him, not caring to discuss the Ardmore's pregnant daughter.

Jacob Watson grinned. "Don't bother yourself, Pastor. I been prayed for already, and I'm getting out of here Tuesday, a well man. You know why? Those women laid hands on me and prayed the Lord would turn me inside out and scrape out those ulcers and all that trash I been carrying around for years, and you know what? He did! I'm a changed man. Like new, boy, like new!"

Andrew mumbled something and said he guessed he'd be going then. Mr. Watson tossed him a final bouquet. "Finally got myself a family, boy. Going to move the Ardmore family in with me. The church will have to wait awhile for my money. Going to need that for my grandson's education!"

That welcome news removed all Andrew's desire for a drive in the mountains, and he headed back to church, picking the thorns out of his "bouquet."

CHAPTER FIFTEEN

Andrew=Apostle of Christ

ANDREW ENTERED the church office building, finding it deserted. Miss Maxom and Patti Barnum had gone home. Tom Packney and old Mr. Walters had the offices clean and neat. Carlo Entini wasn't practicing at the organ this evening, and absolute quiet reigned. Andrew closed his office door, turned on his desk light and sat down to think. What a day! What a week! Was it possible he'd only been in this church five months? It seemed like five centuries.

He got out a piece of paper and a pen and wrote down names, happenings, dates — a thing he used to do in college when he was facing an exam and wasn't sure he had everything in sequential order. He called it "diary-doodling." In a way it was like a diary. It helped bring things into focus, at the same time it refreshed his memory.

On the lined yellow paper he wrote:

—January, entered Bellview Pres. with a light heart
—Nervous Nellie for a secretary (heart of gold)

    –V O I C E S!
    –Nervous Mahoney (examined state of affairs at BPC)
    –Church in the red, stymied, stalemate, why?
    –Mixed up congregation — us/them, ins/outs
    –WHAT'S WRONG W. THIS CHURCH?
    –voices–who, where, why, when, what. WHAT?
    –Queried session, what's wrong? a) extremism b) no
     commitment c) church not alive d) nobody cares. why?
    –then came ABORTION! oh-boy, should have stayed in
     bed!
    –Finally saw them . . . . . MiCe, mIcE, mice, MICE!
    –Dr., sec., think I'm nuts
    –I think I'm nuts!
    –My protagonists (the Charismatics) chasm-atics? make
     themselves known
    –Thorn in the flesh appears (festers!)
    –more Charismatics-more thorn-more MICE.
    –HELP!? help me GOD!

"Dear God," it was more thinking out loud than praying.
"Dear God, here it is May. Outside this window, the trees
and flowers are budding. The grass is greening up. Why am I
so brown and shriveled inside? I don't understand what I'm
doing wrong. I thought I was doing everything right. God,
what's the matter?

"God, who put that book on my desk? Did you? Did you
send all those plagues on me? Am I wrong in your eyes, too?
Oh, Lord, it all seemed so simple in seminary; in my first
church — thousands of years ago in Texas. Then I had faith.
I believed if I tried to do your will, I *would* do your will.
Now I don't even know what that will is.

"God, is your will and your truth what I learned in
seminary? Is it what I taught my students in divinity school?
Is it your will that I suffer the slings and arrows of a pint-sized
pundit?

"Heavenly Father, I'm going to talk to you right now like
I've never talked before. I admit that I'm helpless — at the
bottom of the barrel — down and out for the count of ten.
Please stop the fight! I'm bleeding on the inside!

"Oh, God, you're so far away, and I can't even see the face
of Jesus. Is He still there? God, I don't doubt my salvation. If
I died tonight I'm sure you'd take me to heaven, but if I live
till tomorrow, it'll be pure hell because I'm separated from
you, and I can't get back — "

"You can get back, Andrew."

It was a deeper voice than he'd heard before. It made him
think of Abraham seeing the ram in the thicket.

"Are you Abraham?"

"No."

"Are you God?"

"No."

Andrew had his head in his hands, staring at the top of his
polished desk. The desk light shone on his red hair like a
copper halo. He asked again.

"Are you God?"

"No, I'm Jeremiah."

"Don't tell me you've come to haunt me just because I
preached from your prophecies last Sunday. My God, that's
not fair! Suppose I'd preached from Exodus, would you have
sent Moses?"

*"Andrew, forgive the familiarity, but I've known you for a
long time, I think. No, I'm not Jeremiah the prophet. I'm
Jeremiah Malachi Mouse. It was revealed to my son, Peter,
that I would be the one who would lead you to a renewed
life."*

"Is your son a disciple?"

*"Oh, yes, all my children are disciples. No, that's not right
— John Mark is still out in the wilderness, but Peter,
Timothy, Phoebe, Baby Mary and my dear wife, Priscilla,*

are all filled with God's Holy Spirit and are in His love and care; in His grace and in His will."

"You're a lucky man, Jeremiah. That is, you're a lucky mouse. Why can't I see you? I can hear you well enough. You have a fine voice, a good delivery. But I can't see you."

Jeremiah at this moment had to take a giant step in faith. He was safe enough in the wastebasket. If he suddenly leaped on Dr. Mahoney's desk or his shoulder, what would keep that gentleman from slapping him into a trap or trouncing him with that big brass bookend? For just a moment Jeremiah hesitated, thinking about his family. Then he remembered the words he'd read so many times by the pilot light on the church kitchen stove: "Go ye into all the world and preach the gospel to all men . . . and lo, I am with you always . . . he who confesses me before men, him will I confess before the Father . . . where two or three are gathered in My Name, there I am also . . . ask and ye shall receive."

"But my God shall supply all your need according to his riches in glory by Christ Jesus." These last words Jeremiah spoke aloud, as he vaulted from the wastebasket to the brown leather letter box on the pastor's desk.

Finally, Andrew Pinkham Mahoney, DD, and Jeremiah Malachi Mouse, CCM (Charismatic Church Mouse), met face to face. Jeremiah extended a clean, well-manicured paw, and the minister took it in one of his big, freckled hands. Gently.

"I'm honored to make your acquaintance, Jeremiah," said he, and meant it sincerely. With great dignity, the gray-clad mouse made a low bow. He wore a starched white shirt with an old-fashioned wing collar, a cream-colored waistcoat, and a black bow tie. The gray suit had a tail-coat, three tails, in fact: two of fabric and one of mouse skin. He held a well-worn miniature King James Bible in his left paw.

"What was that verse you quoted as you sprang up on my

desk, Jeremiah?" Andrew was beginning to relax for the first time since he'd arrived at BPC.

"Philippians 4:19; 'but my God shall supply all your need according to his riches in glory by Christ Jesus.'"

"You know I have a need, then?"

"Yes, Andrew, I've been aware of that for some time."

"I believe in God. I believe that I have Jesus Christ in me from the time I accepted Him for my salvation and was baptized. I was sixteen when that happened, Jeremiah. If I have all that, what can I lack? Oh, I'll admit something is lacking. I'm about ready to throw in the towel."

"Dear friend Andrew, have ye received the Holy Spirit since ye believed? Acts 19:2."

"Jeremiah, I know that verse, and yes, I feel I have received the Holy Spirit since I believed. You're not a Charismatic mouse, are you?"

"If I must have a label, sir, that's as good as any." Jeremiah looked the minister straight in the eye. Flashing blue eyes met thoughtful mouse brown ones. Neither flinched.

Andrew began to drum on the table with his fingers. He bit his lip. He tapped his foot against the wastebasket.

"You're trying to tell me that I need to be Charismatic, is that it? You're implying that all the far-out things I read in that book somebody put on my desk are what I need to help me out of this mess. Is that it?"

Jeremiah opened his KJV and pointed to Acts 1:8. "But ye shall receive power, after that the Holy Ghost is come upon you: and ye shall be witnesses unto me both in Jerusalem, and in all Judea, and in Samaria, and unto the uttermost part of the earth."

Andrew opened the Living Bible. He read aloud. "But when the Holy Spirit has come upon you, you will receive power to testify about me with great effect, to the people in

Jerusalem, throughout Judea, in Samaria, and to the ends of the earth, about my death and resurrection."

"I am bold enough to state, and that humbly," said Jeremiah, "that what your ministry is lacking is *power*. You lack power! True, the Holy Spirit dwelleth in you since your baptism unto repentance, but my dear, learned theological friend, you haven't willed that it be released, activated. You've been power-packed all this time but have been missing a spark plug. That's your *will*. The very minute you decide to give everything to God, give him your will so he can work his will in you, then you'll zoom into orbit! That's a Packneyism."

"Jeremiah, does Tom Packney have this, what did you call it, 'release of the Spirit'?"

"Yes, sir, that he does."

"And Miss Hanlon?"

"Yes, sir."

"Who else in BPC, Jeremiah? Has everybody got it but me? Am I the only one out of step?"

"It's not so much that you're out of step, Pastor, as it is you haven't caught up to the music. Some of us have been marching to a New Song only just a short time. My whole family (save John Mark) are renewed. Your secretaries, Miss Maxom and Miss Barnum. Several of your elders and deacons. Many folks from denominations besides this one. Miss Maxom's new friend, the minister at Linwood Street Baptist across the way is Spirit-filled. I believe she's planning to marry him."

"That milquetoast!"

"I'm not sure that's worthy of you, Pastor."

"You're right, Jeremiah. I'm sorry. By the way, would you care to sit down? It can't be too comfortable standing in that letter box." At Jeremiah's nod, Andrew took a small pillow from the couch and put it on the desk. Jeremiah hopped up and placed his Bible beside him.

Andrew stretched his legs a bit and leaned back in his chair. He was feeling wonderfully relaxed and at ease.

"If you've heard my sermons, Jeremiah, you'll know that what I've been trying to do is bring unity to this church by leveling off the Charismatic gifts that tend to make some Christians feel superior — to level off those gifts and make them equal to the natural gifts that God has endowed other of his people with. Gifts that serve the church in many ways, but not so spectacularly. Do you understand this?"

"Sure, Pastor, I understand your intention, but I don't agree that everything has to be leveled off equal. Otherwise, why should we strive for God's supernatural gifts? Why not be content with whatever He's given us in the way of natural talent? But the main point I think you're missing is this . . ." Jeremiah took a deep breath and plunged into the icy waters of Andrew's logic.

"Did you ever see or drive through fields of flat plains? They're uninteresting and monotonous to the eye." Jeremiah had studied geography for years, though he'd never traveled beyond Newark, New Jersey. "Once you've leveled off the mountains you no longer have mountains and valleys but flatness. And Reverend Mahoney, that's where the streams are the sweetest and coolest — in the valleys between the mountains. That's when God can work with us best. In the valleys. Turn to Psalm 104, and look at verse 8."

While Andrew found his place, Jeremiah started to read aloud. His eyes were strong, requiring no glasses. He read eloquently.

"This is my favorite version, though my son Peter likes the one you have. This goes: 'They go up by the mountains; they go down by the valleys unto the place which thou hast founded for them.' And in verse 10: 'He sendeth the springs into the valleys, which run among the hills.' And it is there, Pastor, that you'll find the springs of living water the Bible speaks about. When you've come down off the mountaintop of your intellect and logic and down into the valley of surrender and humility. . . ." Suddenly Jeremiah was aghast at his temerity in so instructing this tall man of God. How dare he, a lowly creature of the living God, presume to advise someone who was created only slightly lower than the angels?

As though a lighted marquee flashed before his eyes, Jeremiah saw the words he'd heard Peter read from the Living Bible at morning devotions: "Then He (Jesus) was filled with the joy of the Holy Spirit and said, 'I praise you, O Father, Lord of heaven and earth, for hiding these things from the intellectuals and worldly wise and for revealing them to those who are as trusting as little children.' " The mouse father whispered a small prayer of thanks for Luke 10:21 as he hopped down from the pillow and laid a paw gently on the minister's wrist.

"Maybe you'd like to read something more from the Holy Scriptures, Pastor, and think on these things for a bit."

"Yes, I think I would, Jeremiah."

His little furry friend replied, "Take your time. Even rabbits stop eating clover, once in a while, to chew things over."

"Ah, friend mouse, you're something of a poet, as well as a prophet."

"Quite so. And now, if you'll excuse me, I intend to meditate upon the Scriptures myself. I pray that God will illuminate His Word to you."

Jeremiah, for whom courtesy was second nature, bowed and made his exit with great dignity. He climbed to his habitat on the top shelf of the minister's closet, and there behind Volumes VII–VIII of the Minutes of the Session, he opened his Bible to the Psalms, and read by the light that came through a crack in the door. It had been an exciting and tiring day. He soon fell asleep.

Jeremiah was aroused from his nap by a knock at the minister's door. Deep in thought and meditation, Andrew didn't hear the knock. It came again, louder this time.

"Oh, Lord," Jeremiah prayed. "Let this be someone with a spiritual flashlight!"

"Thank you, Lord," he said, when he heard the voice of Elder Jim Logan.

"I wasn't sure you'd still be here, Andrew, but I wanted to pick up the evangelism report you had for me. I'm lucky you're working late."

"Sit down, Jim," the minister greeted his visitor. "You are just the man I want to see. Tell me about the Baptism in the Holy Spirit."

Through the partially open door, Jeremiah could see the look of surprise and joy that came over Jim Logan's face as the tall, soft-spoken elder took a chair by the desk. He picked up the Bible and pointed out some passages which he and Andrew discussed. They were talking so softly, Jeremiah could hardly hear their conversation. He was forced to clamber down to the Financial Reports in order to hear.

The two men were praying. Jeremiah's conscience would allow him to eavesdrop no further, so he, too, began to pray. Soon he was caught up in the joy of praying to his Heavenly Father in the language of the Spirit and completely forgot the two men. The minister's voice rose, interrupting the mouse's prayer.

"You know what's really holding me back, Jim? I'm scared. Afraid everything will change. I'm afraid I won't feel the same, think the same, act the same. And this is all I've known for years — the security of sound theology based on fact. I'm not the emotional type, never was."

"Of course you'll change, Andrew," Jim Logan replied.

"How could you not? You'll be a new man! You'll be God's man, not Mahoney's."

It was then that Andrew felt the full impact of all the prayers that had been prayed for him. He felt himself uplifted and held before the Lord God, presented as it were, face to face with his Maker, and he had no choice but to stand there, naked, shivering and afraid.

He bowed his head, his stubborn red head that had for so long been independently erect.

"I know you're right, Jim. Pray with me."

The two men knelt beside the desk. Andrew prayed. "Father, thank you for sending someone to show me the way home. Thank you, Father, that I finally saw myself as I am — all head and no heart. Father, forgive me. I'm ready at last to lay it all before you and work according to your will, not mine. From this time on, let me be filled with your Spirit, with your love and mercy. Grant me all the blessings and gifts you deem right and necessary for me. Thank you, Lord. Praise your name."

Jim Logan laid his hand on Andrew's mop of red hair. He prayed. "Blessed Jesus, fill this man to overflowing with your Holy Spirit. I count it a joy and a blessing to be here as he receives the abundant life, the living water, in your name. Amen."

Even as the Holy Spirit came upon the minister, the mouse in the closet danced in exultant joy before the Lord. Jeremiah turned cartwheels on the shelf. He ran up one wall, across the ceiling and down the other side. Singing in a high falsetto, "It is done! It is done!", he did an elaborate pirouette on his left back leg. Just as he flung his arms overhead and made a broad leap for a *grand jeté*, he lost his balance and fell to the floor. Landing conveniently near his favorite mouse hole, he danced out with a Psalm of David on his lips.

"Who can utter the mighty doings of the Lord, or show forth all his praises? Praise the Lord! Praise, O praise the Lord!"

Andrew Mahoney rose from his knees and embraced Elder Logan. They sang the first verse of "Amazing Grace" and went out together.

Before Andrew could close and lock the door of his office, another small figure entered silently from the darkness of the hall.

CHAPTER SIXTEEN

Of Mice and Ministers

JIM LOGAN went to the parking lot with Andrew Mahoney, while Jeremiah took the path that led to the side door of the church kitchen. He slipped into the mouse hole that led to the stairs and hallway by the kitchen. He hoped Priscilla would have the kettle boiling for tea. She'd be glad to hear the good news he was bursting with. So would the children. He remembered the phrase he'd heard on the television in the lounge. "Do you know where your children are right now?" No, he knew not where young John Mark was, and his heart was sore. He prayed a silent prayer for his protection and safe return.

Just as Jeremiah mounted the top stair leading down to the kitchen level, he heard a heavy thud and a sharp cry of pain somewhere in the darkness ahead of him. He flew down the remaining stairs and grabbed Timothy's flashlight which always hung beside the last step. The small, piercing beam of light showed him that his friend Reginald Rat had fallen into an overlooked mousetrap, the last of Mahoney's Folly. Reginald's sciatic leg was twisted, and he appeared to be unconscious. Jeremiah called out for Priscilla and the children to help him. They all tumbled out of the kitchen door. Phoebe mounted a chair and switched on the overhead light.

"Uncle Reggie!" she screamed.

"Help me get him out of the trap, Timothy and Peter. Let's put him in the kitchen on one of Mother's pillows." It took the three of them, directed by Jeremiah, to get him out of the trap and into the warm kitchen. Reginald hadn't yet regained consciousness but was moaning under his breath.

"Lord, he's a big rat!" said Peter.

Reginald opened his eyes and gave his rescuers a withering glance. His raspy voice was like saw blades over cement.

"Don't just stand there, dummies. Start praying! I'm in big pain, *big* pain!"

"Oh, Lord," said Peter, "he is a big rat, and he has fallen mightily. May we gather round and call for your blessings and mercy upon him."

All the mice gathered around Uncle Reggie and laid their paws on him. Jeremiah, head of the mouse clan, prayed the official prayer.

"Father of all creatures on this earth, in the sea and in the air, we call this day blessed that one of your creatures is knocking at the door of your mercy and forgiveness." He looked Reginald square in the eye.

"Reggie, do you herewith repent of your sins and your sometimes obnoxious habits, and turn to the Lord Jesus as your Savior?"

"I do."

"Do you believe that the God who can save you is the God who can heal you?"

"I do."

"Repeat after me. O Lord, I am truly sorry for all my sins and ask forgiveness. (Pause) I will try to walk steadfastly in your path henceforth. (Pause) I would be baptized with water and with the Spirit." Reginald Archibald Rat repeated loud and clear the words his friend spoke.

"And now, O Lord, I declare, in the name of your son Jesus, that Reggie's leg is healed, both from sciatica and from mousetrapica. Now and forevermore. As you have said, ask and it shall be given. Rise up, Reggie, and walk in the name of Jesus."

Reggie rose up and walked to the nearest cracker box. He sat down. "Praise the Lord! You forgot something."

"What did I forget, Reggie?"

"You forgot to pray for this hacking cough of mine. Might as well go whole hog and be all healed as well as holy."

Timothy spoke up. "Uncle Reggie, I think you have to make an effort on your part as well. I believe you have to be willing to give up your pipe before the Lord will heal your cough."

"Does it say that in the Bible?" Reginald wanted proof-positive before he gave away his last remaining pipe.

It was Priscilla who chimed in. "Our bodies are a temple unto the Lord, Reggie, and you surely wouldn't smoke in God's temple!"

"I never thought of that, Priscilla." He handed her the Sherlock Holmes pipe. "Here, put it in the garbage."

They all prayed for the healing of Reggie's cough. He leaned back on the cracker box, started to put his feet on the white tablecloth, thought better of it and said, "Why don't we all sing a hymn of praise before we have our tea and cakes?"

"Yes, why don't we?" smiled Priscilla as she cut the apricot pound cake in small slices. "And you might give Reggie a drop of that brandy Uncle Caspar sent us for Easter, dear."

"Hold it, Jerry, my friend." Reggie held up a big hairy paw. "Don't need it, myself. But I could go for a few drops of that molasses you had before. Praise the Lord!"

"Praise the Lord!" said Peter, as he led the company of mice in a stirring rendition of "Praise God from whom all blessings flow; praise Him all creatures here below. Praise Him above ye heavenly host; Praise Father, Son and Holy Ghost. Amen."

Priscilla saw that it was quite dark outside, and she mentioned that John Mark hadn't been seen since lunch time.

"Couldn't some of you go and look for him, my dear?" She spoke softly to Jeremiah so as not to awaken Baby Mary.

Jeremiah spoke to each in turn. "Timothy, you check the offices and vacant rooms to see if John Mark is around anywhere. Peter, you look in at the Mousecoteque and see if he's been there. Phoebe, look carefully around the church grounds for John or his Mike. Yes, you may take Timothy's flashlight, but hurry back once you've all looked."

"Ah, Jerry, old man," it was Reginald laying a furry paw on Jeremiah's shoulder and giving him a warm embrace that smacked of tobacco and *Evening in Hardware Store.* Jeremiah wasn't sure he was going to like Reggie as a Christian friend any better than he did as a pagan adversary. "Let me, Jerry, old friend, patrol the street in back of the Pharmacy and the Hardware Store. Perhaps the young fellow may be back there with his friends. I want to get a walk anyway and try out my leg. Oh, joy! It's great to have a decent leg again!" He sauntered out the door, but no sooner was he out of sight than he broke into a trot and finally was able to do the one thing he'd always wanted most to do: jump in the air and kick his heels together. Oh, the Lord was good!

No one found John Mark because he was safely inside the minister's study. Being small, it took him a long while to

accomplish what he needed to do. First he had to upturn the wastebasket and push it over near the pastor's top, left-hand desk drawer. Then, by standing on the basket, he managed to pull open the drawer. But it kept sliding shut, and he was breathless from trying to hold it open. Finally he managed to wedge a pencil in the opening so it wouldn't close completely.

Another trip down to the floor, and he gingerly hoisted his package to the top of the desk and unwrapped it. By opening the drawer wide with one paw, flicking the pencil away with the other, he used his feet to slide the object gently into the drawer. Then, by sitting on the drawer handle with his head in the drawer, he could see to adjust the position of the trap which he'd put in. His simple little plan was just to catch the minister in his own trap (one that he'd found in the closet).

When Dr. Mahoney opened the left-hand drawer to get something, the mousetrap would get him. And that, John Mark figured, would square him with the minister for all the pain and grief the family had suffered at his hands. At the same time it would punish his mother, father, brothers and sisters for making him feel like an outsider. Or so it seemed to him at the time he set up the trap.

He had to work by the light of a small flashlight he'd borrowed from a friend, and by the time he'd returned the wastebasket to its place, a half-hour had elapsed. Then, in order to get out, he slipped the latch open at the top of the window, pushed, tugged and shoved a book under it so that he could escape. Another ten or fifteen minutes went by.

Once outside, he began to be scared. Where to go now? If he went home, his father would surely thrash him. If he went to the Mousecoteque he doubted if he could appear his old casual self. Finally he did something many prodigals have done before — went home, slipped into his bed and went to sleep.

There Priscilla found him when she turned down the covers for Timothy and Peter, who would soon be back tired and weary. Priscilla knelt down by John Mark's matchbox bed and thanked God for returning him safely. Having no one to send out to tell the searchers that the lost was found, Priscilla had to stay with Baby Mary and wait for them. They, in turn, were patrolling the streets, alleys, stores and all parts of the church building.

About nine-thirty that night, Peter saw the pastor's car enter the parking lot again. He and Timothy stood in the shadows to let him pass. They hadn't yet heard the story of his experience from their father, because the excitement of

Reggie's healing and salvation had cast all thoughts of it from Jeremiah's mind. So they still considered him an alien.

Andrew had returned to the church because he was burning to read more from the books and Bibles in his study. He wanted to think about this wonderful thing that had happened to him in the spot where it had happened.

He turned on the hall light and made for his office door. He unlocked the door, threw it open and put his arm out to turn on the light, when he heard a snapping sound, a cry of pain and a curse. The light flicked on, and he saw a youth sitting behind his desk, left hand in a drawer, the right holding a gun.

Andrew took a step forward, the gun went off and the minister felt a sharp, burning pain in his left shoulder. As he fell to the floor, he saw the young man flee through an open window in back of the desk, a mousetrap dangling from the fingers of his left hand. The overhead light swam into a thousand pools of brightness, as Andrew slowly lost consciousness. A spreading pool of blood stained the gold carpet where he lay.

Jeremiah, entering the hallway by Miss Maxom's office, heard the shot and ran as quickly as he could to see what had happened. Timothy and Peter also heard the shot as they were circling, looking once more for their brother. They scampered over the open window sill just as their father entered from the hall.

"What happened, boys?"

"We heard a shot, Father, and saw someone running just as we rounded the corner here by Dr. Mahoney's office. Is he hurt bad?" Peter did the talking, as Timothy had turned squeamish at the sight of the blood-stained carpet and thought he might be sick.

Jeremiah took command. "Here, Timothy, straighten up and get the rescue squad on the phone. This bullet's got to come out of his shoulder. It's in deep. And you, Peter, let's lay our paws on him and pray for his recovery."

Two unexpected visitors appeared in the doorway: Tom Packney and Elizabeth Hanlon. For a moment they couldn't credit the scene before their eyes. The Padre lying on the floor, not moving, blood oozing from a hole in his shoulder and being ministered to by two mice. A third mouse was dialing the telephone. Stunned though he was, Tom Packney reacted typically. "What did you do to the Padre? Who hurt him?" He didn't expect the mice to answer.

Jeremiah was still in charge. "Young man, don't just stand there, beating your gums. Help my son get that call through to the rescue squad and then join us here on the floor for prayer. Your pastor's been shot by a prowler he caught in his office, and we must cover him with prayer and a blanket, if you please, Miss. There's one in that closet on the second shelf."

Tom, Bibs and the kneeling mice had scarcely got their prayers said when the rescue squad appeared. Jeremiah felt he and his sons had done all they could do so they quietly moved away from Andrew and into the closet. The police arrived and Bibs and Tom told them all they knew of what happened.

Miss Hanlon sat at the pastor's desk making telephone calls from a church directory to Miss Maxom, Jim Logan, Bill Gordon and several others. The policeman asked her to telephone elsewhere as they had important work to do in the room.

Bibs smiled. "I'm finished, Sergeant. Just wanted to activate the hot line." She and Tom left for the hospital. Jeremiah, Timothy and Peter walked slowly back to their hideaway in the kitchen closet. Priscilla met them at the door with the news that John Mark was at home and in bed.

"I can't help wondering if John had anything to do with tonight's happenings," said Jeremiah. "Reggie falls into a trap, when they're all supposed to be gone. Dr. Mahoney gets shot in his own office for who knows what reason. I think I'll walk over to the police station and listen in on their report. Maybe the culprit will be caught by now. Yea and verily, man is born to trouble as the sparks fly upward, but Praise the Lord! a man was born again tonight. And so was a creature!"

He met Reggie in the parking lot, and they strolled over to the police station together. In the short space of half an hour the police had taken into custody the prowler, his gun and the mousetrap. The two old friends went back to their homes to wait and pray.

A little after midnight, Andrew was brought from the recovery room at Marlinberg Hospital to a room on the fourth floor. He was groggy and sick but the sight that met his eyes as the orderly wheeled him into his room brought a big smile to his face. Twenty people stood in a semi-circle around his bed singing "The Doxology." He saw Miriam Maxom, Reverend "Milquetoast", Tom and Bibs, several of his parishioners and several strangers. He realized that these were the people who had prayed him into the Baptism in the Holy Spirit, and now they were praying him back into his pulpit.

A wave of his hand and a weak "Praise the Lord!" was all he could manage before the nurse shooed them all out. He loved the look on their faces, when they heard him Praise the Lord! And of course, they didn't know yet . . . or did they? One thing Andrew knew for sure, beyond the shadow of a doubt, was that the love these people had for him was real and warm, and he could feel it covering him like a mantle. On that joyous note, he fell asleep.

CHAPTER SEVENTEEN

The Littlest Prodigal

ON THEIR way home from the hospital, Tom and Bibs were discussing the minister's accident and wondered if they might have imagined the part about the mice.

"We'd have missed the whole thing, Bibs, if you hadn't suddenly had the urge to confess to the Padre and ask his forgiveness," Tom said.

"I have another confession to make, Tom," and Bibs told him she had seen and heard a feminine mouse, lavender-frosted, talking and working the mimeo machine in the church office when she interviewed Dr. Mahoney.

"But I just put it down to nervous exhaustion. I didn't want to believe I'd actually heard a mouse talk. This must be the same family."

"Yeah, but Bibs honey, we don't have to *say* we talked with three mice, do we? Couldn't we just keep this to ourselves?"

"We can try. Remember how funny Sergeant Patrick

looked when he asked if we found Dr. Mahoney, and you told him the mice did? I thought for a minute he was going to arrest you for being stoned."

"Yeah, I'm sure he thought we were dumb teen-agers."

"Tom, do you remember that the biggest mouse told us to lay hands on Dr. Mahoney and help them pray? Did I imagine that or did it really happen?"

"It happened, Bibs, and I don't know when I've heard a more sincere prayer. If it's possible, and I guess anything is possible in our Father's world, I'd say those were Spirit-filled mice. What do you think?"

"Biblically and doctrinally and theologically, it probably couldn't happen. But He created all things, so who knows? You're right, though; we really should keep this to ourselves."

They stopped at the police station as the sergeant had requested them to do. Thinking it over, he really could have arrested them, and maybe he would even now. But the sergeant was not at all interested in bringing charges against Tom and Bibs, and was glad to have the news that the pastor was doing well and would recover. He told them they had arrested a young man in the neighborhood carrying a gun and a mousetrap.

"As near as I can figure it," Sergeant Patrick said, "this young man was on the prowl for money and stuck his hand in the pastor's desk drawer which contained a loaded mouse-trap. When dr. Mahoney switched on the light and surprised him, the thief had just caught his fingers in the trap and reacted by pulling the trigger."

He invited the two young people to sit down. He continued. "Speaking of mousetraps, as we were, how was it you told me you didn't find the pastor, but the mice did? You weren't by some chance connected with the mousetrap episode, were you?"

Tom answered, "Oh no, Sergeant Patrick. You see, I work at the church as part-time custodian after school, and I know the Padre, er ah, the pastor was all upset about hearing mice on the premises. Mostly in his office, I think. He had old Mr. Walters — he's the senior custodian and almost deaf — he had old Mr. Walters set out a bunch of traps all over the place. All baited with cheese. Far as I know he never caught a single mouse, but the cheese always disappeared. Never could figure that one out."

After this long explanation, far more than the sergeant wanted, Tom had a brilliant thought. "Hey, Bibs, you don't think the mice put that trap in the Padre's drawer just to get even with him?"

Bibs said nothing. The sergeant said, while making notes on a paper, "Young man, if you're trying to be funny, don't! And let me say right now," he pointed his yellow pencil at the two young people, "don't leave town! You'll be needed as material witnesses when this case comes to trial. Unless, of course, you'd like the mice to testify for you."

The sergeant dismissed Tom and Bibs, and they started home, sleepy and tired. Bibs knew her parents would be worried in spite of the quick call she had made to them from the hospital. It hadn't occurred to her to ask them to join the prayer group at Dr. Mahoney's room, since they didn't yet see the same truth their daughter had seen.

"Bibs, I'm coming down here to church as soon as I can after school, and see if I can find that Papa Mouse. If he really talked, then he really thinks, and he'll want to know how the Padre is. And then — there's that bit about the trap in the drawer. I just don't believe an intelligent man would put a mousetrap in his own drawer. Too much chance he'd forget it and wham!"

"Well, Sherlock, I've got news for you: this is Saturday,

and there's no school! Boy, am I glad. Call me later and let
me know how the Padre is. He's a great guy, really. I just had
him figured wrong. I think he's got the baptism."

Tom grinned at the pretty blonde with the blue eyes and
the Prince Valiant haircut. Tom was glad Bibs had come to
accept the Padre as her friend, too. He still couldn't believe
that Elizabeth Lorraine Hanlon was going out with him.
Praise the Lord for fringe benefits!

When Tom got to church about nine o'clock that
morning, he found Miss Maxom already there. She had
called the hospital to see how Dr. Mahoney had rested
during the night and found that he had slept well and was
sitting up in bed having breakfast.

Then she turned to Tom. "Well, Praise the Lord, Tom,
Andrew is doing just great. Isn't that wonderful?"

"Sure is, Miss Maxom. Say, do you know anything about
mice being connected with this case in any way?" He
watched her carefully to see how she would take this
information. She didn't bat an eye.

"Oh, by all means. But they've been praying for Dr.
Mahoney; they wouldn't put a trap in his desk, if that's what
you mean. What makes you ask?"

Tom told her what he and Bibs had seen when they
stopped in at the pastor's office late Friday.

"Why don't we go and ask them?" Miriam got up to lead
the way.

"You know where they stay? You talk to them?" Tom
found all this very hard to swallow. "We must all be cracking
up. Even Bibs saw a purple-streaked one the day she typed
the Padre's sermon."

"That would be Phoebe," said Miriam. She told Tom about the entire mouse family, as they walked to the kitchen. Miriam knelt down and rapped gently on the cabinet door. Priscilla answered her knock.

"Good morning, Priscilla. Tom and I wanted to speak to Jeremiah, if he's around."

"You'll find him on the side lawn under the oak tree. He's interrogating our young John Mark. I do hope he hasn't been in trouble."

"I wouldn't worry, Mrs. Mouse. I'm sure John Mark hasn't done anything bad. By the way, the hospital said that Dr. Mahoney had a good night and was eating breakfast."

"That's a blessing, Miss Maxom. The Lord is good."

The prim little mousewife wiped her eyes on her blue-flowered apron and turned away from the door. Tom and Miriam went out the side door to the church yard. Under the huge, old oak tree sat a young mouse wearing faded blue mouse-jeans and a T-shirt emblazoned with a large Number Seven. Facing him under the tree sat his father, Jeremiah Malachi Mouse and a rather large rat who was chewing gum. Jeremiah welcomed them and explained the situation. He was dealing with several minor and one or two major transgressions committed by the young mouse.

After John Mark confessed to the transgressions, his father forgave him and gave his arm a pat.

"Aren't you forgetting an item of particular importance to this case?" The gum-chewing rat adjusted his cap and picked up a twig from the ground to put between his teeth. He was pleased that the Lord had delivered him from smoking a pipe but he still needed something to chew on, so a twig and chewing gum sufficed for the time being.

Hope they don't get mixed up together, Tom was thinking. Just then Jeremiah stopped to introduce the two people to the neighbor from the Hardware Store.

"Reginald, I haven't forgotten a thing," he replied to Reggie's question. "But I propose to do this in my own way, if you don't mind." Reggie fell silent and added another twig to his mouth.

John Mark now confessed that it was he who had put the trap in Andrew Mahoney's desk. The teen mouse seemed about to cry. "So I guess it's all my fault. I only meant to teach him a lesson, I didn't mean for him to get shot. What will they do to me?"

Jeremiah was in a dilemma. He didn't honestly know what course of action to take. Was John Mark in effect guilty of wounding the Reverend Mahoney because his trap had startled the prowler into shooting? Would the thief have pulled the trigger anyway? He tried some scripture.

"Thou shalt not kill."

Reginald rejoined with, "An eye for an eye and a tooth for a tooth."

"Honor thy father and thy mother," it was John Mark's attempt to tell his father he loved him. "I was trying to avenge us for the traps the pastor laid for us."

"Vengeance is mine, saith the Lord," his father replied.

Tom Packney, sitting on the grass with Miss Maxom, interrupted.

"Beg your pardon, Mr. Mouse, but you're never going to get anywhere this way. Somebody can always find a Scripture that shows his viewpoint if he tries. Speaking as a teen-ager, I believe your son is only guilty of playing a prank on the Padre. John Mark had no earthly way of knowing that somebody would break in. The thief was probably trying to find money to buy drugs. If he hadn't meant to use the gun, he wouldn't have had it."

"But I left the window open a crack when I got out," came a further confession from the young culprit.

"Ah, John, my son," sighed his father. "There was a mouse hole in the closet."

"I think —" said Reginald.

"What do you think, Miss Maxom?" Jeremiah asked.

"I agree with Tom. I'm sure Dr. Mahoney will in no way blame your son. He himself was guilty of setting at least four dozen traps with the express intention of catching your family."

"An eye for an eye and a tooth for a tooth," Reginald tried again.

"Were none of your family ever caught?" Miriam asked.

"Only one, my daughter Phoebe, but she was healed. The Lord gave us special protection."

"But that's the way He caught me," Reginald said, a note of pride in his voice. "If it hadn't been for that trap, I mightn't be on the Lord's side today, and I'd still be hacking and coughing and limping. Praise the name of the Lord!"

Reginald stood up and drew a small blue box from his waistcoat pocket. He handed it to Jeremiah.

"A little token of my esteem. In grateful appreciation of I Samuel 6:4,5 and 18."

Surprised, Jeremiah opened the small box and gasped. There in a bed of gray silk lay a miniature golden mouse, with topaz eyes and spectacles! He showed it to Miriam and Tom.

"Why, Reggie, this is really the nicest thing anybody ever did for me. I'm sincerely flattered. But where on earth did you find a golden mouse after the manner of I Samuel 6:4,5 and 18?"

"From the Avon lady!" [6] said his bosom friend. "And now I'm off to mid-morning Bible study. Good day to you all, Christians." So saying, Reginald Archibald Rat tipped his cap, made a semi-bow and strolled out into the morning sunshine. He had all he could do to refrain from executing a mid-air kick, his now favorite way of showing his thanks to the Lord.

Tom Packney had the last word and the decisive one. "Mr. Mouse, sir, I don't think this need go any further, except to tell Dr. Mahoney when he gets back. I'll tell you why: if you attempt to tell the sergeant at the police station, he won't be able to hear you. He's not gaited that way. And it's for darn sure I'm not going to tell him. He already half-thinks I'm a nut, because I mentioned that you mice were there when we found the Padre. We could leave him an anonymous note, but that wouldn't hold up in court and anyway, who ever heard of a mouse trying to trap a minister? Why the General Assembly would have fits. They like to think their preachers are in charge of things, and it wouldn't do for them to think mice were putting their oar in.

"No, I see no other alternative. Naturally, the Padre, being the just and kind man that he is, will forgive your son's prank and let that be an end to it." Tom stood up and held out a hand to the secretary.

"Before you go," squeaked the changing voice of John Mark, "would you all pray for me to be like my father, my mother, my brothers and sisters? I just can't stand to be an outsider anymore. Can I have a little place in the Lord's family?"

"Oh, errant son of mine," his father blew his nose on an oak leaf. "You've always had a place in the Lord's family. It was only waiting for you to claim it. Shall we pray?"

The mailman, wheeling his cart down the drive by the side of the church building saw a strange sight. Two people and two mice, kneeling, all with heads bowed. He vowed that the minute he got back to the post office, he would call Dr. Abernathy for an appointment.

"I thought my feet would go first, but here it's my head that's caved in. Oh, me!"

CHAPTER EIGHTEEN

Gathering the Remnant

ELDER JIM LOGAN preached the sermon, while Dr. Mahoney was in the Hospital. All the parishioners knew that the minister had been shot, but few knew he'd been reborn. The following Sunday, Andrew was back in the pulpit. He entered the sanctuary from the anteroom behind the organ as Carlo Entini sailed through a Saint-Saëns prelude. The choir and congregation sang an opening hymn of praise, and the student assistant read from the Psalms and led the opening worship.

Andrew stood to his full height, both arms upraised. His voice was like a trumpet.

"Let's praise the Lord!"

He was delighted to hear many people respond with "Praise the Lord!" and "Amen!" He gave a deep chuckle, and crossed his arms, laying a hand on each of his shoulders to show them that he was indeed well again.

"My friends, how good it is to see you this morning."

There on the front row on his left sat Miss Maxom with a Jewish couple, strangers to Andrew but not to Jesus Christ. Alongside her were Tom, Bibs and their friends. His elders and deacons were lined up on the next three pews. In the front row right sat Emily Ardmore, her husband, daughter Monica and old Jacob Watson. Behind them sat Dr. Heggel. The downstairs was filled and half of the balcony. Straining his eyes just a little, Andrew could make out seven mice figures on the farthest balcony railing. Priscilla, Jeremiah and their offspring, glowing like golden mice in the eleven o'clock sunshine. Andrew chuckled again. He had never felt so happy in his life.

"Friends, this is a celebration to the glory of God for his great and mighty works to all his creatures and to glorify his Son Jesus." He opened his Bible. "I shall read from Jeremiah 23, verses one through six, in the King James Bible. It is my confession to you."

"Woe be unto the pastors that destroy and scatter the sheep of my pasture! saith the Lord.

"Therefore thus saith the Lord God of Israel against the pastors that feed my people; ye have scattered my flock and driven them away, and have not visited them; behold I will visit upon you the evil of your doings, saith the Lord.

"And I will gather the remnant of my flock out of all countries whither I have driven them, and will bring them again to their folds; and they shall be fruitful and increase.

"And I will set up shepherds over them which shall feed them: and they shall fear no more, nor be dismayed, neither shall they be lacking, saith the Lord.

"Behold, the days come, saith the Lord, that I will raise unto David a righteous Branch, and a King shall reign and prosper, and shall execute judgment and justice in the earth.

"In his days Judah shall be saved, and Israel shall dwell safely; and this is his name whereby he shall be called, THE LORD OUR RIGHTEOUSNESS."

Andrew began his sermon, "Dearly beloved of the Lord . . ." Jeremiah whispered proudly in his wife's ear, "He's beginning to talk the way I do!" His wife squeezed his paw and smiled.

"Dearly beloved of the Lord," the minister said again. "Although the words I've just read are from the prophet Jeremiah, I am certain the Lord God meant them for me. I am guilty on all counts. In January a brash and worldly man stood before you, presuming to take you to task for failure of this congregation to grow — in numbers and in dollars. When you failed to do either of those things, I presumed to judge you of little faith and to cut back many services normally rendered by a shepherd to his flock. Is it any wonder that you scattered?

"So the Lord said, 'Ye have scattered my flock and driven them away, and have not visited them: behold, I will visit upon you the evil of your doings.' What the Lord said He would do, He did! Because I judged you, He judged me.

"But I was judging you for something that was no fault of yours. How could you give, when you had not received? How can a body grow, when its diet is insufficient? Heaven knows, I couldn't supply you with a full complement of spiritual vitamins and minerals, because I didn't know the MDR — the minimum daily requirement.

"I couldn't furnish you with spiritual meat and bread, because I was eating Pablum myself!

"I could in no way offer to quench your thirst with living water, because I, too, was in the desert.

"As one of you so kindly told me after my first sermon, my predecessor always preached from the Bible, never from the New York *Times*! And I believe you've been hearing the

Gospel. Furthermore, I believe I've preached the Gospel — sometimes! And then only as I knew it. But my dearest friends, you were not hearing the *full* Gospel, and I wasn't preaching the *full* Gospel, because we didn't know there was more to preach and to hear.

"Is there more, you ask? You can bet your bottom dollar there's more! And I have finally found the source of supply; finally learned the MDR; finally located the springs in the valley where the living waters flow."

Andrew closed his notebook, picked up his Bible and stepped to the center of the chancel, standing on the top step in the middle of the aisle.

"Let me tell you how the 'evil of my doings came upon me', and how the Lord God redeemed the time I've frivolously wasted in berating his saints."

He strode about, lifting his Bible aloft, telling with great merriment how the plagues fell upon him. "It all started the night I ran out of gas, left my car on the street, and it was *spirited* away to Newark." Here he laughed out loud. Next he told about the frozen pipes that burst.

"But I was looking for living water, not frozen water. *That* I had plenty of!"

"Then my tires began mysteriously to go flat; two in the front on Monday. Two in the rear, on Tuesday and so on throughout the week.

"They will never, ever speak to me again at the Gulf Station. But to paraphrase a familiar saying of Jesus, 'I have fuel ye know not of!'

"Then came the voices. Did you ever hear voices? Everywhere I turned I heard still, small voices, so much so that I was convinced we had churchmice and had dozens of traps set to catch them."

The congregation laughed heartily. Clearly, they didn't give credence to talking mice in the church building.

"Bats in his belfry, more like," murmured Carlo Entini to himself.

"I didn't catch the mice, but I caught plenty of trouble. Several families left the church. An elder sued to recover his church pledge — and won! Committees and board members were at each other's throats and mine.

"Then somebody said, 'The Charismatics are coming!' To a dedicated, unemotional intellectual like myself, that was tantamount to yelling 'Fire!' in the sanctuary. For that's exactly what it was — *fire!* The fire of Pentecost. But praise be to God, the church isn't burning down — it's burning *up!*"

Andrew paused briefly to gaze out over the congregation. He smiled again. How I love you one and all, he thought. Why not tell them so? He did.

He spread his arms wide and said, "How I love you one and all! I love you because you first loved me. Because you led me face-to-face to the One who is All Love." He paused and blinked back a tear.

"After I'd fought the Charismatics to a standstill, or so I thought, I discovered that they had all been praying for me for months. And Friday night, two weeks ago, I sat downstairs in my study and told the Lord I couldn't go on fighting any longer. I wanted Him to stop the fight — I was down and out.

"And that's when one of God's own creatures explained to me what was missing in my life. Joy and power! The joy and the power of that part of the Trinity that I'd been guilty of selling short for so long.

"My friend said to me, quoting St. Paul in Acts 19:2; 'Have ye received the Holy Spirit since ye believed?' And he told what it meant to be baptized in the Holy Spirit, and what it meant in his life.

"I prayed to receive God's Holy Spirit in all its fullness,

and I know I will never be the same again. At first, I didn't
feel very different, just peaceful. I just accepted the fact that
I had received the Holy Spirit's release of power when I
asked. Then in the hospital, I read the Bible as never before,
because the words just seemed to jump out and come alive.
It's like having twenty-twenty vision times two: X-ray eyes! I
had to tell somebody about it, so I told the nurses, the
doctors, the orderlies. You know what, some of them already
had it! The others called me a 'charisma-tick', and I just
laughed. I've been laughing for days! I'm laughing now
because I feel just like old Scrooge must have felt when he
discovered that he wasn't chained to the spirits of Christmas
Past and Christmas Future — was no longer dead but living!

"I sing and pray in a beautiful language of the Spirit of the
Almighty God, and I have never been so happy in my life
before!"

Andrew laid his Bible on the chancel step and started
walking down the aisle, greeting first one then another with a
hug, a handshake, a kiss. When he finally returned to the
chancel, wiping his eyes, many people were laughing or crying
and embracing one another.

Andrew held up his hand. "It was said of Scrooge, ever
afterward, that he knew how to keep Christmas. I hope it
may be said of Andrew Mahoney that he knows how to give
Christianity away. I want to share this joy, show you what I
and others have found. Oh, I hope you will receive it, for it's
the greatest Gift of all. It's at long last to put Christ, the
Lord of Righteousness, at the center of one's life; and that
dear friends, is very Heaven!

"Today we won't take up a collection. We may not take
one next Sunday, either. You may bring your offerings up, if
you wish, and put them in the plates here on the chancel
steps, but only if you truly feel that you can bring yourself
with it. By this action I hope you will say to our Lord and

Savior: 'Jesus, I do now rededicate and reconsecrate my life to you, both now and evermore. To walk in your way and do God's will.'

"If there be any among you who wish to ask for the baptism in the Holy Spirit, please remain here with me at the chancel. This is not to be a dividing of our ranks but a uniting of ourselves as one in the Spirit, held together in the bond of peace. If you feel this is not for you, we bless you and love you anyway.

"But as old Scrooge, when his nightmare was over, flung wide the window to let in the golden, heavenly sunlight, so shall you who ask, receive in glorious abundance the joy, the power and the peace of a spiritual New Day! Let us pray.

"Holy Father, we thank you and praise your name for the wonderful gift of your Son Jesus and for the empowering of our lives by your Holy Spirit. Thank you for giving me a new life. Thank you, too, for using me to help rehabilitate the young man who shot me. Lead him, by your grace and mercy, into your kingdom. Receive now our gifts and ourselves as we come before you in love and rededication. We are all your children, Father; all your creation. In Jesus' name. Amen."

Carlo Entini, recovering slowly from the shock of the morning, swung softly into "Amazing Grace," as the choir and the people took up the words. Andrew, tears of joy streaming down his cheeks, glanced up at the balcony and blew a kiss in the direction of Jeremiah and his family. A few people left their seats and walked directly out the front door. Many more came, embraced Andrew Mahoney, and remained at his side. It was a New Day for Bellview Presbyterian Church.

Afterword

🖋 I NEVER thought of writing a story about church-mice, until I dreamed one night I had already done so; after that, I couldn't get it out of my mind. A whole family of mice just seemed to move in, bag and baggage, and the thing got underway. It was to be about the renewal of a church as seen through the eyes of a mouse family. Not a children's story except in the sense that we are all children — children of God.

After the first few chapters when they had established their identity, they started turning up in odd places. Jeremiah and Peter (stuffed, of course) were found in a restaurant. Lavender-frosted Phoebe sat in a drugstore waiting to be taken home. Reginald's "token of esteem" was written into the story months before I saw it in a catalog.

So you see, from starting out as a device, they ended up as directors. From speaking for the little people in the church, the laymen, they began to speak for themselves, as well. If they bear any resemblance to other churchmice, I'm sure they'll resent it deeply and it's purely coincidence on my part. The people, it must be understood, are all fictional. The mice are oh, so real!

After reading their story I had to laugh at the presumption of a housewife dipping into theology and parrying scripture as though expert. Then God showed me that He, too, has a sense of humor, for I was directed immediately to Acts 17:30. "And the times of this ignorance God winked at." I'm sure He loves us all, mice included.

It was comforting to read from George Macdonald: "Let the heartless scoff, the unjust despise! The heart that cries Abba, Father, cries to the God of the sparrow and the oxen; nor can hope go too far in hoping what God will do for the creation that now groaneth and travaileth in pain because our higher birth is delayed." C. S. Lewis, *George Macdonald,*[7] *an Anthology*; Macmillan, 1948.

Also comforting is Ecclesiastes 3:21 in the Living Bible: "For who can prove that the spirit of man goes upward and the spirit of animals goes downward into dust?"

Our man in the mousetrap says, "Hearken, O people, if you start hearing voices or develop indigestion while reading these pages, it behooveth thee to reach for the Bible instead of the bicarb!" — Jeremiah Malachi Mouse.

Wynelle B. Gardner

* * *

I *have* to catch Folly today; it's time to stop being so feeble. She needs her hooves picked out, and if I bring her in and give her a feed and a groom then maybe I can try getting back whatever bit of trust she used to have in me. After all, she is *my* horse. It's only a couple of weeks since it gave me a thrill to say that, instead of a prickly chill. I take a carrot and hide the headcollar around my back. The ponies are too busy grazing at the bottom of the field to take any notice of me. Folly's in her favourite place under the tree. I walk over slowly, remembering for the first time in ages the time I spent with her at Doris's, before I messed up. She walks towards me. I think she smells the carrot. She stretches out her head to it and lifts her top lip. I slip the headcollar around from behind my back, but quick as a flash she lunges at me with her teeth, then strikes out with a front hoof. I catch it on the knee.

It's over so quickly that Folly's down the other end of the field with the ponies before I realize what's happened.

It could be worse. The bite on my arm hasn't broken the skin – luckily I have my coat on. It's just a deep purplish nip. The kick hurts more. I roll up the leg of my jeans and explore my kneecap. It's turning pink, and it's raw to the touch, but everything moves the way it's meant to.

The carrot and headcollar are lying on the ground. I pick up the headcollar and leave the carrot. I head back up the field towards the gate, headcollar over my shoulder, ignoring the swelling in my throat and the back of my hand when I was fourteen. That was quite deep too. Mum didn't notice.

"Oh," I say. I yawn. At least not having a girlfriend or any friends means I can go to bed straight after dinner – that's if Mum intends to make any dinner.

"So they're keeping her in to see how she goes. She's running a temperature too. Only Stacey thinks they're only using that as an excuse because they won't let her go home until social services have been to check up on her."

That gets my interest. "What's it got to do with social services?"

"Och, probably nothing. She's just panicking."

"What about Cian?"

Mum purses up her mouth. "She's not speaking to him. She says she can't trust herself. Oh, he was all apologies last night – I went in with her, it was near three, and he was sitting there blurting and sad and looking for sympathy, but she just said she couldn't listen to him."

"I think he *is* sorry."

"You're not taking his side, are you? Leaving a six-year-old to look after a three-year-old!"

"Yeah, but would you leave *him* to babysit? He's high as a kite half the time. Seriously, Mum, the kid's got real problems. What did Stacey expect? It's partly her own fault."

"Och, Declan, that's not fair."

Maybe it's not. I don't know; I don't really care. I'm fed up with the subject. I'm fed up with *every* subject. And tomorrow is just going to be more of the same. Only worse.

pain in my knee. I try to whistle.

"Hiya!" It's Sally, on her way up from the bottom field with Nudge. She glances at the headcollar. "Have you just turned Folly out? I haven't seen her for ages – or you. Is your head OK again? You look a bit pale."

"I'm fine, thanks."

"How's Folly getting on?"

"Fine." I can't admit to Sally that Folly hates me, that I've done something to her that I can't remember and she won't forget, that under my clothes bruises are darkening as proof of this hatred.

Could do with a bullet, that thing.

* * *

"Declan," says Mum. "Run over to Stacey's with this, love, would you? I don't want to miss the start of *EastEnders*."

I sigh but take the Tesco's bag.

"It's just a few wee things I got her when I was doing the groceries. Sure God love her."

It's not so long since Mum couldn't even manage to do her own shopping, let alone anybody else's.

I ring the bell on Stacey's door and nearly die when it's opened by Seaneen. She looks mortified too. Her cheeks flame and she swallows before she speaks; I can see her throat move.

"Oh," she says. "Hello." She stands with her hand on her belly.

"Um." I hold out the bag. My voice comes out funny. "Mum sent this."

Courtney prances up the hall. She's dressed for clubbing. "Declan!" she shrieks. "Me and Seaneen's watching *Hannah Montana*. Do you want to watch it with us?"

Seaneen looks away.

"Uh, no, I have to go, Courtney. Sorry."

"Awwww!" She hangs on to Seaneen's sweater and looks up at her. "Declan's my friend. He minded me."

"That's nice," says Seaneen. She looks at me properly for the first time. Her eyes are huge. "Stacey's at the hospital," she says. "She asked me to babysit. Courtney, go on in and keep watching – you can tell me what I've missed when I get back."

"Awww." Courtney pouts but she trots off obediently.

"Where's Cian?" I ask.

Seaneen jerks her head upwards. "In his room. She doesn't trust him to babysit. For obvious reasons."

"So do you still feel sorry for him?"

Seaneen wrinkles her nose in a way that makes the freckles join together. "Ah, you know – a bit. I saw him earlier coming out of the bathroom. He looked awful. Like everything was too much." She lowers her voice. "Stacey's scared of social services getting involved – with Madison getting hurt like that – and she blames him. Did you hear he stole her phone and sold it?"

"To pay off Emmet?" I remember the "business" he said he was doing the other night.

"I dunno. Because Cathal said, when I was in the shop today, that Emmet's still looking for him. Anyway." She chews her lip. "I better go and see what Courtney's up to."

She has the door closed before I can even say